Memories

Memories of Sun

of Sun

STORIES OF
AFRICA AND AMERICA
EDITED BY JANE KURTZ

Amistad

GREENWILLOW BOOKS
An Imprint of HarperCollins*Publishers*

Memories of Sun: Stories of Africa and America
Copyright © 2004 by Jane Kurtz

"an african american" copyright © 1990 by Meri Nana-Ama
Danquah. First published in *The Hollywood Review*.
Reprinted by permission of Meri Nana-Ama Danquah.

"My Brother's Heart" adapted from *Of Beetles and Angels* by
Mawi Asgedom. Copyright © 2001, 2002 by Mawi
Asgedom. Reprinted by permission of megadee books and
Little, Brown and Company, (Inc.).

The text of this book is set in Adobe Garamond.
Book design by Chad Beckerman

Library of Congress Cataloging-in-Publication Data
Memories of sun : stories of Africa and America / edited by
Jane Kurtz.
    p. cm.
"Greenwillow Books."
Summary: A collection of short stories and poems by authors
from both continents about life in various African countries
and some of the experiences and impressions of Americans in
Africa and of Africans in America.
ISBN 0-06-051050-1 (trade).
ISBN 0-06-051051-X (lib. bdg.)
1. Africa—Literary collections. [1. Africa—Literary
collections.] I. Kurtz, Jane.
PZ5.M546 2004 808.8'0326—dc21 2003049067

First Edition 10 9 8 7 6 5 4 3 2 1

 Greenwillow Books

FOR THE CHILDREN OF AFRICA—SOME
OF WHOM WERE MY CHILDHOOD
FRIENDS, SOME OF WHOM I'VE RECENTLY
MET IN UGANDA, KENYA, NIGERIA,
ETHIOPIA, AND THE UNITED STATES

—J. K.

Contents

Introduction • 1

AFRICA

Bagamoya
by Nikki Grimes • 9

Ella's Dunes
by Elana Bregin • 13

Scenes in a Roman Theater
by Elsa Marston • 39

October Sunrise
by Monica Arac de Nyeko • 59

Kamau's Finish
by Muthoni Muchemi • 75

AMERICANS IN AFRICA

Into the Maghreb
by Lindsey Clark • 89

Our Song
by Angela Johnson • 95

The Homecoming
by Maretha Maartens • 107

What I Did on My Summer Safari
by Stephanie Stuve-Bodeen • 137

Her Mother's Monkey
by Amy Bronwen Zemser • 149

AFRICANS IN AMERICA

an african american
by Meri Nana-Ama Danquah • 169

My Brother's Heart
by Mawi Asgedom • 175

Flimflam
by Jane Kurtz • 189

Soldiers of the Stone
by Uko Bendi Udo • 203

Lying Down with the Lion
by Sonia Levitin • 227

About the Authors • 245

Introduction

IN THE BEGINNING, ACCORDING TO SCIENTISTS WHO have been studying human DNA, a small, sturdy group of people walked out of Africa. From there, human beings eventually spread all over the earth. Dr. Spencer Wells, a population geneticist who has studied and conducted research at Harvard, Stanford, and Oxford Universities, says, "We are all African under the skin."

This news comes as no surprise to me. Every time my jet airplane lands in Africa, I have powerful feelings of coming home. When I'm away, I hoard my memories of the intense African sun, the acacia trees, the animals, the people. Then again, I landed in East Africa for the very first time when I was only two years old. My father—at that point a young man who had grown up on a farm in eastern Oregon—and my mother—then a young woman who had spent her childhood moving from one small Iowa town to another—had decided to leave the United States to work for the Presbyterian Church in Ethiopia. For more than thirty years, members of my family would live and work in East Africa. I grew up as someone who is sometimes labeled a "third-culture kid," a person who doesn't fully belong in her parents' culture but doesn't fully belong in the culture around her, either. Third-culture kids struggle to figure out just where they do belong.

Mine was the first family to be issued an Ethiopian visa after World War II. I'm sure my parents made quite a stir when they arrived, lugging three young children. (And my mom was pregnant.) I spent most of my childhood near a remote southwestern village called Maji. Before the airplane could land on the savanna, it had to buzz low to get the ostriches and zebras and antelopes out of the way. Then we climbed into a jeep and rode all day, thirty-two bumpy miles up the mountain.

Maji was a magical place to grow up, but my family, a

nurse, and a teacher were the only people there who spoke English and although I knew enough Amharic to play with my friends, I often found myself in the middle of conversations (either in Amharic or one of the other Ethiopian languages) where I was lost. Sometimes life in Maji scared me: when my father would inoculate mules against sleeping sickness, the mules kicking and squirming, the men shouting, holding them down; or the time a friend took me on his shoulders and waded out into the middle of a funeral dance where I was surrounded by ceremonial spears shaking all around me. The year I was seven, my parents said we were going "home" to visit the United States. I thought all my feelings of being an outsider would finally go away.

After we reached our New York hotel, my mom told my sisters and me, "We're going downstairs to get something to eat. Remember that we're in America now. Be sure to use your forks." A little while later, we were all perched on stools at a counter, eating. My mom glanced at her four daughters and then tried to pass a discreet order down the line. "Tell Jane she can eat her potato chips with her fingers." When the message reached me, I blared in a loud voice, "Which ARE the potato chips?"

As everyone turned around to stare, my heart trumpeted

the news to me that I was an outsider in the United States. Later, I spent a stiff eighth-grade year in a junior high in Pasadena, California. When I was introduced as the girl who was from Ethiopia, someone would always ask, "Did you see Tarzan?" By the time I came to the United States a third time—for college—I was convinced that there was no way to talk about Africa.

After many years, though, I found my voice . . . through my writing. I've written a number of stories connected with Africa—folktales, historical fiction, contemporary fiction, nonfiction. I also do a great deal of speaking at schools and conferences. As I talk with people, I notice that although we are all African under the skin, many in the United States still find the continent that birthed humankind, in the words of a recent news report, "distant and dangerous."

This anthology of short stories offers glimpses into contemporary Africa. It also explores questions about borders: What happens in those interesting places where cultures meet? My life taught me that cultural connection is often tough and sometimes impossible. But from my family I learned that it was important to approach cultural differences with humor, curiosity, and respect, or, in the words of the poet W.H. Auden, to do your best to "love your crooked neighbor with your crooked heart."

Some of the authors whose stories are in this collection live in Africa. Some live in the United States. And some are "third-culture kids" engaged in a lifelong quest to find out just where they do belong.

—Jane Kurtz

AFRICA

Bagamoya

BY NIKKI GRIMES

Candle-lit seaport
its breezes sigh hotly
with the romance of
remembered greatness
the old days of long ships
and trade
before the Red Sea
brought bandits
and body snatchers.

Still the flavor remains
mud-house and moonlight,
gnarled tree trunks
with overhung branches
slithering snakes
and whispers of magic—
witches abounding.

Oooooooh, Bagamoya
Oooooooh, Bagamoya town
Huendi Bagamoya, Mama,
said the teacher.
Stay away from Bagamoya town.

Shrouded old women dance
in legless silence
down the roads of Bagamoya.
I have seen, he said.
What? What have you seen? I asked.
Ahhh! At night, these women,
these Black ones . . .
they are too full of Power, he said.
Unasemji? I asked.
I say, these women
are too full of power.
They turn people
into cats, said the teacher.
I laughed
to shame him, I thought.

Then, one night,
I awoke sweat soaked,
to blown-out candle
and midnight silence
shattered by
a wail of cats in chorus
grim and chilling
and calling my name.

Ooooooooh, Bagamoya
Ooooooooh, Bagamoya town—

Ella's Dunes

BY ELANA BREGIN

"IT'S ONLY FOR TWO WEEKS." MY MOTHER FLUFFED HER hair with her scarlet-tipped fingers. "It'll do you good to spend some time with your father for a change."

"But I don't know him," I protested. "I haven't seen him since I was six!"

"All the more reason why you should get reacquainted now."

I fiddled with my lucky crystal pendant. "You always said such bad things about him. Now you want me to like him. Just because it suits you. So you can dump me there while you and your boyfriend go on vacation together."

I stared resentfully out the window at the traffic whizzing by. We were on our way to the bus station so I could catch the Intercity up to the Northern Province, where my father would fetch me and drive me out to his place in the hills. "You'll like the Magaliesberg," my mother said as if I hadn't spoken. "It's a beautiful area. And the Bushman Farm sounds interesting."

"What is a Bushman Farm, anyway?"

"Some kind of tourist thing," my mother said vaguely, checking her lips in the rearview mirror. "All I know is that there are Bushmen there and tourists come to see them and learn about how they used to live."

"Sounds like a zoo." I'd studied the Bushmen in school. Our textbook called them "an ancient Stone Age people," which made them sound about a million years old. They were supposed to be the first inhabitants of South Africa, who roamed the desert and mountain regions, living by hunting animals and gathering plants. They were small, used poisoned arrows, and did lots of rock paintings in mountain caves. The early settlers had killed off most of them. I hadn't even known till now that there were any living Bushmen left at all.

We were only just in time for the bus . . . as usual. Punctuality is not my mother's strong point. "Have a good time with the Bullfrog," I said, watching the driver stow my luggage.

"Oh, Annette. Do you have to call him that?"

"I can't help it if that's what he reminds me of. Anyway, he calls me White Mouse and I hate that."

"It's just his way of being friendly, darling. Would it kill you to be nice back?" She made a reproachful mouth at me and leaned in for a hug, keeping space between us so that I wouldn't crease her blouse. My mother's the only person I know who can hug without touching. I climbed on the bus and turned to wave at her through the window. But there was just empty pavement where she'd been standing. She hadn't even waited for me to find my seat.

The countryside rolled by, plowed fields where flocks of white birds rose and fell like bits of paper. There were rocky hills and sparkling rivers and slopes covered in wild grass with toy-sized cows dotted across them. I thought a lot about my father, worrying about how I would recognize him after all this time. My mother and he had divorced when I was six. I'd gotten a postcard once, from somewhere called the Kalahari, which looked like the middle of nowhere. The picture showed a line of big, dark buck with long V-shaped horns, crossing red dunes. The writing said: "Dear Annette, this is where I'm living now. Hope you are well. Love from your dad."

My mother said the buck were called gemsbok and the place was a game park in the Kalahari, where my father was working as a tourist guide. I wanted to know more. But I didn't dare ask, in case it got her moaning about him again. I already knew all her complaints by heart.

As it turned out, I needn't have worried about recognizing him. He was the only one waiting at my stop. And I was the only one getting off. "Annette?" He peered at me from under his bush hat with flaps down the sides. "You've grown up!"

We shook hands awkwardly, like the strangers we were. I'd forgotten how tall he was, how blue his eyes were. His face was tanned, full of lines and creases from the sun. He looked a lot older than my mother did.

I climbed into the van with SAN ROCK: BUSHMAN CRAFT AND CULTURE FARM stenciled on the side. Above the writing was a logo of a crouching Bushman in a loincloth, holding a drawn bow. My father and I rode mainly in silence. I stole a glance at his face that was familiar and yet not familiar. He seemed stern and distant; I couldn't imagine him tucking me up in bed at night.

"I hope you won't be too lonely here," my father said, breaking his long silence as we turned in at the sign that said WELCOME TO SAN ROCK and bounced up the unpaved road that led toward the line of looming hills. "I'll be busy with tours in the day. But I'm sure you'll find things to interest you."

"The Bushmen?" I blurted.

He glanced at me in surprise. "What about them?"

"Can I meet them?"

"Of course!" He smiled. "They're keen to meet you. I've already told them that you're coming." I felt a small thrill that they should know of my existence. "You'll like them," he added. "They're lovely people. Very friendly."

I stared out the window at the view of patchy dry grass and low bushy trees that stretched away on either side of us. Two diminutive figures bobbed toward us through the glare and shadows of the bushes. They trotted barefoot through the hot and thorn-strewn dust, moving in effortless rhythm, as graceful as antelope.

"Is that them?" I asked breathlessly.

"Who?" My father's gaze followed mine. "Oh, the Bushmen. Ya. That's Ella and the little one is her brother Yakob."

He honked to get their attention. They veered obediently toward our truck.

I saw now that the girl was older than I'd first thought,

about fourteen—my own age. It was her small, light build that made her look younger. She had a beautiful face, wide at the cheekbones, pointed at the chin, with deep-set eyes that curved like bird's wings, almost lidless, so that they seemed to look straight out from the soul inside. Her hair was parted into neat plaited rows drawn tight against her skull. Everything about her seemed graceful to me. Full of magic. Her little brother stood beside her, small and shy. They seemed so light, as if their bones were made of air, as if they could blow away like birds into the sky at any minute. I was afraid to breathe too hard, in case I made them vanish.

Ella kept her eyes downcast while my father introduced us, speaking in Afrikaans, which surprised me. Yakob smiled shyly and squirmed away to hide behind his sister. Her eyes lifted to me just once. But in that brief glance, I knew they'd seen all they needed to. A white mouse. White hair, white skin, pink nose where the sun had caught it. No magic in me at all.

"Don't they speak English?" I asked my father as they walked away from us.

"No," he said. "And it's a big problem for them here. Their home tongue is Nama. But they also know Afrikaans, because that's what people speak in the Cape. You can speak it, can't you?" He glanced at me. "Don't you learn it at school?"

We did. But I'd never taken much interest. I was sorry now.

"Is that where they're from? The Cape?" I asked him.

He nodded. "I got to know them when I worked down there. They're Cape Kalahari Bushmen, the last survivors. Among the few left who still have knowledge of the old ways. The tragedy is that they're losing that knowledge fast. Without land of their own to live on, they can't survive."

"Why do you call them Bushmen?" I asked him. "Aren't they San people?"

He grimaced. "Ya, that's the popular term now. But they prefer the old name. They say that San is what others call them."

I had a thousand more questions to ask him. But we had arrived. The dirt road ended in a wide gravel parking lot shaded by big flowering trees. In front of us was a thatched building of stone with a wide wooden deck running along the outside. There were wooden tables and benches placed invitingly in the shade, lots of flowerpots and flower boxes, painted with bright African designs.

"Here we are. Welcome to San Rock." My father gave me a rare smile.

I stood blinking in the hot sun. The dry bushy hills of the Magaliesberg stretched in a long line against the horizon, gray and green under the blue sky.

"Are you hungry?" he asked. "Would you like something to eat?" I shook my head. "Well, anytime you want, just order from the restaurant. Should I show you to your room, so you can unpack?"

My room was across the lawn, a little round hut with a roof of thatch and walls of rough plaster. It was cozy, and I liked the view of the hills from the window.

"Will you be all right if I leave you?" my father asked, edging toward the door. "I have to get to work, I'm afraid. There'll be tour parties arriving any moment. Wander around, make yourself at home. There's a museum and a craft shop and the Rock Art Gallery. And the Bushmen. I'll take you up later to meet them."

He didn't really know what to do with me, I could tell. I was in the way here, just as I was at home.

When I'd finished unpacking, I wandered outside into the singing heat of the day. The sky was full of white clouds, big and fat and puffy. I stared up at the rocky spine of the Magaliesberg hills, wondering if there were caves up there. I remembered there had been famous battles in those hills. Boers fighting British. Or was it black tribes?

Everyone always fighting everyone else. I saw tempting little tracks winding along through the scrub. If I'd had a friend, it would have been fun to go exploring.

I headed across the lawn toward a long thatched building, which the sign outside said was the Bushman Museum. Inside were glass display cases full of big, creamy ostrich eggs, decorated with scenes of antelope, insects, and birds, or long-legged Bushman figures, some with animal heads, running, leaping, crouching, dancing. In one corner of the room, on an island of red sand, was a hut of thatch shaped like a tepee, which a placard said was a "traditional Bushman hut" called a *skerm*. It was surrounded by a whole collection of Bushmen things: long curving wooden bows and slender stone- and bone-tipped arrows. Animal-hide bags and clever little tortoise-shell purses. Necklaces of seedpod; a giraffe's kneecap, used to mix poisons on; even a little floppy puppet doll.

I tried again to remember what I knew about the Bushmen. They hunted with arrows tipped with the poison of snakes, insects, and plants. They carried water in ostrich-egg containers and buried them in the desert so that when drought came, they would have secret stores to sustain them. They knew the desert and the wild animals that lived in it as well as they knew their brothers and sisters. I thought of the girl called Ella. In the Kalahari, where she came from, did her family still live in the old way? Did they still know how to read the tracks of the animals in the sand, find their way across waterless desert, make fire by rubbing sticks together?

I wandered back outside, following the gravel slope of the path up the hill. At the top was a thatched gazebo. Figures were moving there, a small group of adults and children. I saw the shiver of fire, smoke rising faintly, like breath. No one noticed me as I walked up. Men squatted on their haunches around a central fire, heating thin iron rods in the flames and burning charcoal animal shapes onto small squares of wood or bone or bigger slabs of rock. The women sat separately, grouped beside three pointed *skerms*, stringing necklaces from beads of seed-pod and bone. They all had the look of Ella—the same slight build, light honey-colored skin, wide faces, and deep eyes. Their hair stuck up in twisted knots or was plaited to the skull, as Ella's was, or dangled in tendrils from under flowered *doeks*. One of the women was very old, her face full of deep cracks, like the dry clay surface of desert water pans.

My presence was suddenly noticed. The group froze in surprise, exclaiming to one another in a rapid language full of rich and popping clicks. I saw Ella staring from her distance. A short, slight man came over to me. He wore long trousers and an anorak, despite the heat. His feet were bare, and on his head was a cap of fur made from a jackal's head, the snout resting oddly on his forehead.

"Are you Baas Pieter's daughter?" he asked me in Afrikaans.

I nodded bashfully, not sure of my welcome here.

He looked me over with shrewd, attentive eyes. "My name is Abel, but in my language they call me Groot Kat—Big Cat. Do you know why?" I shook my head. "Because I'm such a good hunter!" His wink made me a co-conspirator. When he smiled, all his wrinkles smiled with him. "Come, Pieter's daughter," he said. "Sit down here."

He dusted off a thin plank bench for me, and I sat down self-consciously. The stares of the women were making me shy. One of them said something to the others, and the whole group laughed with great enjoyment.

Abel grinned at my red face. "You know what they are saying?"

Again I shook my head.

"They say that you are truly the apple from your father's tree."

"Thank you," I mumbled stupidly, not knowing what else to say. There was fresh laughter from the group. The diminutive children giggled, stealing glances at me and whispering behind their hands. Ella was much older than the rest of them. She sat a little apart from the others, tossing up stones and catching them on the back of her hand. Like me, she seemed to belong nowhere. We watched each other without seeming to, our eyes darting away whenever our glances caught.

The little ones started shoving at Yakob, egging him on to something. In a sudden dash, he came zigzagging up to me, gave my ponytail a bold tug, and scampered away again.

"Ow!" I rubbed my scalp in exaggerated pain. As if that was a signal, the whole small giggling mob came rushing at me, yanking pieces of my hair with hard little hands. This time my yelps of pain were real.

Ella scolded them sharply. She gave me a long sideways look. Then, calling her little brother to her, she took off the necklace she wore around her neck and nudged him across to give it to me. It took me a moment to recover from my surprise. "Wait—" I said to Yakob. From my own neck, I took my lucky crystal.

We examined our gifts, both of us smiling. Mine was a small, square pendant of wood with a charcoaled gemsbok, suspended from a beaded leather thong. I put it on with reverence, feeling it nestle into my skin as though it belonged there.

A warning cry sounded from one of the women. A tourist party was headed up the hill toward us, my father's tall figure in the forefront. There was hurried activity all around me. Clothes were stripped off, the cups and pots and other traces of civilization hurriedly swept up and hidden in the *skerms*. Before my eyes, the group transformed themselves into the Stone Age people of the history books. The men wore nothing now but loincloths of animal skin, the women, skirts of animal hide. Abel kept on his jackal-head cap, which made him look oddly ferocious.

The tourists joined us. My father introduced the group by their Nama names, pronouncing the rich popping clicks with ease. He explained that they were real Bushmen, whose real home was in the Kalahari desert, who had come here to sell their crafts and teach people about the Bushman way of life. He pointed out the rows of brown, white, and black necklaces for sale, the slender skillful bows, the rock slabs with their intriguing scenes of Bushman life.

The Bushmen smiled shyly at the gaping visitors. But

Ella's face was sullen and unsmiling. She sat bare-chested like all the women, my crystal pendant oddly out of place between her breasts. The tourists crowded closer, staring.

"Do you have any questions you'd like to ask them?" my father asked. "If you speak Afrikaans, you can talk to them directly. They'll gladly answer your questions." There was silence from the tourists.

"They're very friendly people." My father tried again. "They enjoy talking to visitors and explaining their way of life. They have interesting stories to tell."

"Have they no shame?" a woman asked in English. "How can the women sit like that, exposing themselves in front of everyone?"

"In their culture, breasts are not something to be ashamed of," my father explained. "The shame is ours, not theirs. They see nothing wrong."

The woman didn't seem convinced. Others in the party were fingering the crafts. "How much?" a big man asked my father, looking at a rock slab showing dancing figures around a fire. Above them, rain fell in thick specks from dark clouds.

"Let's ask the artist," said my father. "He can also explain to you what the painting is about. Each of these scenes has its own story."

"This is a very special story," Abel said, in his soft-spoken, lilting Afrikaans. "It shows a Kalahari circle dance. Sometimes in the Kalahari, we dance for rain, sometimes to heal sickness, sometimes to set our spirits free. Here are the women sitting round the fire, clapping and singing. Here are the men in their trance, dancing for rain. And the rain is falling. The desert can drink now. See the grass growing already here? And the animals are coming back, because there is water again."

"Ask him how much it is," the man said to my father, as if Abel wasn't standing right there in front of him. I hated the way Abel seemed to shrink beside his bigness. For a moment, I looked through his eyes, and my heart sank for the Bushmen. It struck me suddenly what little people they were. So misplaced here, with their cracked desert faces, their animal skins and wild forests of hair.

"That was horrible!" I said to my father later as we sat at the outside tables of the restaurant, eating our supper.

"What was?"

"The way those tourists looked at the Bushmen. How can you make them sit there like that, all naked, like primitives? They're not primitives!"

"I don't make them do anything, Annette," he said coldly. "They put on traditional skins because they want to, because they know that's what the tourists pay for. Tourists don't want to see Bushmen dressed in Western clothing, looking like everyone else. They want the Stone Age people with their bows and arrows living wild in nature. That's what they come here to see."

"But they hate it," I insisted. "Ella hates it. You can see she does."

My father said nothing.

"It's wrong to put them on show like that. Like animals to be stared at."

"Annette." My father put down his fork. "Abel and his people came to San Rock of their own free will. They wanted to come—do you know why? Because they knew that it's their best chance of survival. Do you know what kind of life they lead in the Kalahari? Starvation! Complete poverty! Drinking themselves to death. There's nothing else for them there. They have no land, no money, no way of earning a living."

I kept my face deadpan, busily sculpting sand dunes of rice with my fork.

"At least here they have full bellies every night. Their children can go to school. There are regular tourists to sell their crafts to. They don't have to go and stand on a highway in the middle of nowhere, hoping that the occasional speeding car will stop and buy from them."

He shoved food into his mouth, chewed angrily for a while. "Do you think I like putting them on display?" he demanded as if I'd argued further. "I agree with you. They shouldn't be here! Of course they don't belong on a tourist farm! Their place is the Kalahari. They should be given the land back—and that was theirs to begin with—and be left to live on it the way they want. But it's not that simple! There's politics involved. And even if they had the land, they wouldn't be able to survive on it without some way of earning their keep. This is not the old days any-more. Everyone has to pay their way in this mercenary world. The Bushmen are no exception."

It was the most talking I had heard him do. I could hear in his voice how much he cared about them, and a pang of envy went through me.

That night, my hut felt like a dark and lonely cave. It was hot, and the mosquitoes made it hard to sleep. I opened my door and stepped outside. The night throbbed and ticked with countless insect and amphibian voices. The sky shivered with stars, more than I'd ever seen in my life. From the Bushman camp, strange singing drifted down the hill. I drifted up, called like someone in a dream.

The group sat around their hissing fire. They were

singing high, discordant tunes in a language I didn't recognize. Guitars strummed, mingling with the tinny vibration of other instruments. The children slept among them, little blanket-wrapped bundles slumped across the adult laps. Ella shifted up to make space for me, and I squeezed in gratefully beside her. No one else paid any attention to me. No one told me to go. The singing continued without pause. The little warm circle of bodies felt cozy and safe. The fire was a comforting protection against the shadows of the night. Beyond, the great silent mystery of the stars stretched without end.

I must have dozed off, for I woke to find that someone had draped a blanket over my shoulders. The circle was full of gaps; one by one, the sitting figures had wrapped themselves in blankets and lain down to sleep just where they were. I found my space among the smoky humps of bodies. And the next thing I knew, it was morning.

After that, I went up regularly to the Bushman camp, spending as much time as I could there. The Bushmen didn't seem to mind. And neither did my father. I think he was just glad to have me occupied and out of his hair.

Ella and I formed a strange bond. It was a friendship of minimal words, for my poor Afrikaans and her lack of English made conversation exhausting. But we evolved a private language, reading each other's subtle clues like tracks in the sand. I admit I sometimes found her a hard puzzle.

She was as changeable as the weather. Full of fun one moment. Brooding and silent the next. There was a restlessness about her that made me think of a spirit trapped. I learned that Abel and his wife were not her parents. Her parents were in the Kalahari. But they couldn't take care of her. She wouldn't tell me why.

"Do you like it here at San Rock?" I asked her once, in my bad Afrikaans.

Her headshake was immediate. "It's not home. The Kalahari is our home. Not this place. We're going to go back there soon. Abel said so." There was a longing in her face that hurt me. "When I'm back there, you can come and visit me. I'll take you walking on my dunes and show you all the special places. The sand is red there, real sand, not like here. Kalahari sand has a special magic in it."

"What kind of magic?" I asked skeptically.

She gave a shrug. "You'll see. We say that once the sand gets in your shoes, you will always have to come back, because your heart stays there forever."

I'd noticed before the way she always said we, seldom I. As if the group all shared the same thoughts, as if one heart drove them.

"If it's so wonderful there, why did you leave? Why did you come here?" I couldn't resist saying it; but I saw by the way her face closed down that it was the wrong question.

Sometimes Ella and I would go off together and find our own secret place under the stars. She would tell me stories, Kalahari stories, she called them. About star people and animal people and powerful shamans who could change themselves into the shapes of jackals or lions. I didn't understand all of what she said. But I loved the sound of her voice, flickering like honey-colored flame in the darkness. I loved lying with her under the starry sky with the wind of the hills blowing over us, while she pointed out the stars to me by their Bushman names.

The days drifted by, oddly timeless, like the fat white clouds that gathered above the stone hills. I felt as if I had been living this life forever; this was my real life. The other belonged to a different Annette.

"If I wanted to stay here," I said impulsively to my father one night at dinner, "just supposing that I wanted to come and live with you, would you let me?"

He was silent. I could see my question had caught him by surprise. "It's possible, I suppose," he said cautiously. "We could discuss it. Theoretically, I see no reason why not. But what about your mother?"

"She wouldn't care. Too busy being lovey-dovey with the Bullfrog to notice whether I'm there or not."

More silence followed. "What about your school? Aren't you settled there? What about your friends?"

I considered his question, thinking about my school friends, who always had the same opinion on everything. I thought of all the times there wasn't room for me in the carpool group, the parties I wasn't invited to. My friends were people I hung around with, but would they miss me? Would I miss them?

"I'd have friends here," I said. "I'd have Ella. She and I could go to the same school. We could start there together in the new term."

"Ella is doing fine at the school she's at."

"No, she's not. She doesn't even go."

"Of course she goes! I drop her off there myself every morning."

"She doesn't go in," I said. "She told me. They make fun of her there. They call her a stupid Bushman. And the teachers shout at her because she's got no English and she can't do the work."

He stared at me helplessly across the table. "Why didn't I know this? Why did nobody bother to tell me?"

Because you're the Boss, I wanted to say. You think

you're their friend, but you're not. You're just the Boss.

The next day it rained, a soft and misty rain that soaked into the dry dust with a sweet smell. "There'll be no tourists today," Abel predicted. "Tourists don't like the rain."

Everyone seemed to brighten at the thought.

"Come and sit here. I'll do your hair for you," ordered Ella, shoving me down on the plank bench. She wove braids into my hair and twisted them into little knobbly knots that stood up all over my head. Then she marched me behind the *skerms* to change into Bushman dress: a skirt of animal skin like hers, longer at the back, short in the front, leaving my chest bare. The thought of being so naked made me shy. I'd never bared my breasts to anyone. But Ella's eyes held a challenge that I couldn't defy.

I let her strip me, felt the strange, cool texture of the skin skirt against my own skin, fought the urge to cross my arms over my breasts.

"Now you look more Bushman." She nodded approvingly, rubbing dust into my skin to dull its whiteness.

The other Bushmen laughed in delight to see me so transformed. The women embraced me like a sister, leading me over to sit with them. My self-consciousness faded. I felt different from my usual self; lighter, freer. I loved the sensations of wind stirring against my naked body, the warmth of fire against my bare skin, and the soft, moist spray of the rain that blew in under the thatch.

I crawled into one of the *skerms* to see what it felt like. It was a snug space, like the shell of a tortoise. It was made for little people and I just fit. The only way I could get out again was to lie on my back and wriggle out feet first. The Bushmen laughed. I loved their laughter.

The rain drummed harder. They built up the fire, and we sat closer to its warmth, drinking sweet tea out of tin mugs. I listened to the familiar clicking talk around me, breathing deeply the smells of wood smoke, wet dust, and smoked bodies.

The fire spat and shook like the voice of an oracle. A different smell mingled with it now, pungent and strange. A long pipe of bone was being passed around the circle, filled with some burning weed. The smell of it made me feel oddly dreamy. The talking quietened. Hands began to clap in rhythm. There was singing, high and monotonous. The men got up and began to shuffle round the circle in a stamping, hopping kind of dance. Women joined them.

"Come on." Ella pulled me with her into the circle. At first, I stumbled behind her, clumsy and clueless. But then she moved back to stand close behind me, holding my waist so that her hips were pressed to my hips and my legs were forced to move in time with hers. After a while, my feet found the right rhythm. Round and round we went, shuffle shuffle hop, our bare feet stamping in unison into the soft dust. The misty rain closed out the rest of existence. There was nothing in the world but this group, this fire, the beat of clapping hands, and the thin, high voices singing.

For a time, I felt that I drifted out of my body. I soared like a bird over wide stretches of sand. Red dunes rose and fell away beneath me. I saw animals; lines of gemsbok with sharp-horned heads held high, cantering across the steep shelves of sand. Behind them trotted animal-headed hunters, with drawn bows in their hands.

Lightning lashed across the sky. Thunder bellowed. The desert shook, dissolved into misty twilight. Slowly, reluctantly, I came back to myself. The singing and clapping had petered out. The Bushmen were drifting out of the circle to build up the fire, seek out the warmth of blankets. I had no idea how much time had gone by. Around us, a cold evening stood darkly banked against the sodden hills. The rain still poured, turning the world to mist and mud.

I stood close to Ella's warmth, only partly aware of how my body shivered. My spirit was still soaring free in the desert realms of stillness and space. A strange elation filled me. For the first time in my life, I understood what it was to belong. I had no idea how any of it would work out. Whether my father would let me stay on here, whether Ella and I would still be friends tomorrow, or whether the Bushmen would leave San Rock and follow their hearts back to the Kalahari. But tomorrow didn't matter. For the moment, I was here, part of the Bushman family, with Ella, my friend. And this moment was really all that counted.

Scenes in a Roman Theater

BY ELSA MARSTON

WITH A SIGH, HEDI PLUNKED HIMSELF DOWN ON A stone seat in the Roman theater. As the last of the afternoon's tourists straggled off and disappeared among the ancient walls, he stared dully at the grand view of the ruins and the green hills of the Tunisian countryside beyond.

He hadn't done very well today. Only one hat sold. His mother would be disappointed, and he wouldn't blame her . . . having to make those hats every night after her day's labor in the fields, weaving straw till her fingers were sore. Tomorrow he'd try harder. Midwinter break from school gave him a few days to earn money, and he couldn't waste the chance.

It'd be so much better, Hedi often thought, if he could be a guide, more interesting and more money. Once in a while he did manage to latch onto a friendly couple and show them a few sights . . . the temple, the theater, the baths and marketplace—and best of all, the communal toilet where twelve people could sit at a time. That always got a laugh, and Hedi would get a few small coins. But that was all. A real guide had to be older and know a lot more.

So Hedi was stuck selling hats in the ruins of a once-glorious ancient town and wishing he could see something else of the world. His parents held out no hope of that, as year after year they struggled to make a living from two small wheat fields. But Hedi had a plan. In a couple of years he would quit school and go to work in one of the big seaside resorts, like his brother Tawfiq. He let his imagination drift in that direction now . . . an exciting life in a land of fancy hotels, rich people with big cars . . . and money.

His attention snapped back. Two boys, one carrying a couple of straw hats and the other a tray of small souvenir trinkets, were climbing toward him up the theater's worn steps. Tahar and Azouz, schoolmates of Hedi's, an inseparable pair. Approaching, they sneered at his stack of unsold hats.

"Some salesman you are," said Tahar, knocking it over with his foot.

Hedi rescued the hats and tried to give an indifferent shrug as the others sat down near him. They pulled candy bars from their pockets and began to eat ostentatiously without offering him a piece. Tahar and Azouz always did better than Hedi, in school and in the Roman ruins. They knew how to amuse the tourists—or make pests of themselves until their victims bought a hat or an ancient fake just to get rid of them.

Now Hedi noticed two more people entering the theater. Awkwardly laden with various items, they looked purposeful . . . not like tourists. The man set down a small stool and arranged a wooden sticklike contraption. He spoke to the woman and soon left with long-legged strides. The woman looked around as if selecting a view, then placed a white square on the easel, sat down, and started taking things from a large cloth bag. Watching from his stone seat higher up, Hedi understood. Artists liked to paint ruins.

"Here's your chance to sell a hat, Hedi," said Azouz in a mockingly sweet voice. "Or are you too shy?"

41

The words stung Hedi as though he'd been pushed into a cactus. Well, why not try? He'd show those pests. Followed closely by Azouz and Tahar, he hopped down the steps, climbed up on the stage, and approached the woman.

"Chapeau, madame? Très bon, la qualité supérieur . . . " His words faltered as the woman pulled a floppy pink hat from her satchel and put it on. She was Tunisian, of middle age, dressed in jeans and a man's shirt with dabs of color on it. Glancing up at him, she answered in Arabic.

"No, boys, I don't need a hat. Run along now, please, I'm busy."

With effort, Hedi tried again. "Ah, madame, you need a better hat. Look, look at my hats, the very best. Don't buy anything cheap, madame. I assure you these are the best quality—my mother makes them, so I know. They'll keep the sun off, keep your skin nice . . . " He blathered on, conscious of the other boys' smirks.

Azouz and Tahar now pushed Hedi aside and took over. They begged, laughed, bombarded the woman with questions. They pretended to stick their fingers in the paint on her palette and then decorate each other's faces. She smiled slightly at first but soon dropped any pretense of amusement.

"Boys, *yallah*! I have to work. Please!"

Hedi caught the nervous edge to her voice. Not content with goading *him* on, only to show him up as a fool, now Azouz and Tahar were getting under the woman's skin.

Again she protested, her voice rising, but it just inspired them to mimic. Finally, with a huff of exasperation, she took a roll of plastic film from her basket and started to spread it over the paint-laden palette. Hedi watched, feeling more and more prickly. Before he could think twice about it, his indignation boiled over.

"Stop it!" he snapped. "Let her work, or I'll go get the guard." Something in his voice knocked Tahar and Azouz off balance. It startled Hedi as well—he wasn't one to boss other people. But it worked. With sheepish grins, the boys backed off. They picked up their merchandise and started to leave the theater area, scuffing their sneakers to show they were in no hurry.

"Okay, okay," Azouz tossed back. "Don't get mad at us, Hedi. Oh, *please* don't get mad. You scare us."

When they had gone, the artist looked at Hedi uncertainly. *"Merci,"* she murmured, and got back to work.

Unsure what to do next, Hedi stood awkwardly for a moment. Then he said, "I'm sorry. I—we shouldn't have bothered you like that. Those two are idiots."

"An artist meets that sort of thing," she said without turning.

Hedi watched for a few more minutes as she sketched a scene of columns and semicircular rows of seats with her brush. Getting up his courage, he thought of something else to say. "Do you paint for fun? I mean, like a hobby?"

"Well . . . I like it, obviously," said the artist, "but it isn't just for fun. I'm having a big show soon. I'll do two more paintings here at Dougga, and then at a couple of other Roman sites. It takes time. That's why I got upset when . . . " Her voice trailed off as she concentrated on the painting, and Hedi decided he'd better not bother her anymore.

The sun was dropping below an orchard of olive trees that bordered the ruins, making shadows of the stately columns creep across the stage. Already the air was chilly. Hedi gathered up his unsold hats, said good-bye, and trudged out of the theater and through the ancient streets, toward the road that would take him to his village about a kilometer away.

So the artist was coming back. It might be interesting to watch her work, a change at least. But what if those two pests came and bothered her again? Maybe she needed somebody to help her, to protect her from hassling, since it looked like her husband didn't want to stick around. The idea sparked a memory, something Hedi's older brother had said a week or so earlier.

Tawfiq had come home for a day to bring money for the family. At one point he and a friend, with Hedi tagging along, had gone to the village café. The friend wanted to know about Tawfiq's work as a waiter. Was he really making good money?

"You bet! But"—Tawfiq went on after pausing for a sip of his mint-flavored tea—"you earn it, believe me. On your feet all the time, running, and always with a smile on your face. It helps with the tips."

Then he chuckled. "Sometimes I do better by looking tough. There are all kinds of guys hanging around at these big resorts, and foreign women can get hassled. So some nights I wait around the lobby or the gardens, and if the manager sees something like that going on, he gives me the word and I just step in and put an end to it. I've gotten some fat tips, protecting the guests." He rubbed his fingers and thumb together lightly.

Now Hedi considered that word . . . protecting. Well . . . wasn't that what he'd done, in a way, when the boys were pestering the artist lady? Yes, that's what he could do, if she came back: He'd protect her. And she'd probably give him a nice tip, if he did a good job.

The next morning, therefore, as Hedi set out with his hats, the Roman ruins looked a little different to him. They might hold new possibilities . . . a new job, a step closer to the glamorous outside world.

The woman came at noon. Her husband, in a tweed jacket and turtleneck shirt, again helped her get settled on the theater stage. Hedi watched from a spot where he could catch their words, thanks to the good acoustics of the ancient building, and heard the man ask if she wanted him to stay. Evidently reassured, he soon left, promising to return in three hours.

Then Hedi ambled over to her and was pleased to see a look of recognition on her face. "Are you working on the same painting?" he asked.

"No, a new one." She went on as though she welcomed his interest. "I'm doing the theater at different times of day, with different light and shadows, different angles. You can see so much change in just one place, you know, if you really look."

Hedi shrugged. A ruin was a ruin. How could it change?

He set down his stack of hats and said, diffidently, "I—

I'm not too busy today, so I'll stay here to help you. I mean, if you need anything, you can just ask me. Or if anybody bothers you, I'll stop them. So you can work in peace."

She gave him a quizzical smile. "Well, thank you. I don't think I'll need anything, but . . . all right. Just so long as you let me concentrate."

But Hedi wasn't quite willing yet to withdraw. He was frankly curious about a man who would go off and leave his wife by herself. "Your husband . . . *monsieur* . . . he doesn't like to wait here?"

The woman pulled on her paint-smeared shirt, then shook her head. "He brings me from Tunis and then drives to a café in the nearest town and reads. He's a professor; he always has to read."

"It's nice that he lets you paint so much," Hedi said, probing a little deeper.

The artist focused on squeezing her paint tubes until the palette was neatly arranged with blobs of brilliant color. At last she spoke. "It's an important show. My paintings bring very good prices now. I can get whatever . . . we ask. Yes, I suppose you're right. It is nice."

Settling down, Hedi watched as the woman sketched the scene, then precisely and delicately blocked in the colors. Soon he observed that she was painting both what she could see and things she *couldn't* see. There were statues taking form on her canvas, but no statues in the real theater. Nor were there any scarlet cushions left on the stone seats. And look at those ghostly Roman figures floating among the rows, some looking haughty and rich, some bending to chat with friends. Hedi watched, more and more intrigued. So that was what an artist could do—make the world look not just the way it really was, but the way she wished it to!

Now, what could Hedi do to help her? After a while he got up and hustled away to fetch a soda from a man who sold drinks at the entrance to the ruins. When he returned and offered the cold, wet bottle, the woman looked up in surprise.

"Oh . . . thank you, but . . . well, thank you. How much—"

"Nothing, it's just so you won't get thirsty."

She frowned slightly, then took a sip and placed the bottle at her feet. At that moment Hedi heard the babble of an approaching group. He stood up, ready. Sure enough, a large cluster of tourists were entering the theater. A guide spoke to them in loud French, but many soon spotted the artist and hurried over to watch her at work.

Hedi's cue. *"Pardon! S'il vous plaît!"* he said, trying for a firm voice. The visitors looked at him, annoyed and puz-zled. He went on more boldly in French, "Please do not look. The artist must work hard, so please do not bother. She will have an important exhibition. You can see it later." Disgruntled, they drifted back to their group. Hedi saw that the guide had interrupted his speech and was saying something about the artist. All faces, with expres-sions of high interest, turned toward her briefly.

He'd done it—protected the artist! And something else, he realized. For once, he had *told* the foreigners, instead of beseeching and begging.

An hour or so later, Azouz and Tahar came swaggering into the theater. Caught off guard at seeing Hedi with the artist, they paused, which gave him a moment to steel his nerves. He gestured for them to retreat a little and, to his surprise, they did.

"What're you doing here?" said Tahar as Hedi followed them.

"It's a job," he muttered, thinking hard for a plausible explanation. "The theater's reserved for the artist today. I'm in charge."

Azouz sputtered. "*What?* I never heard of—"

"It's a new rule. Go find the tourists someplace else." Hedi turned his back on the other two, hoping his newfound bravado would carry it off, and a moment later he heard their footsteps shuffle away. He couldn't help a little grin.

The artist was starting to clean up when Hedi returned to his post near her. He studied the painting, in which the theater rose partially ruined and partially reconstructed, with figures drifting among the rows of seats and columns.

"That's really good!" he said.

"You like it?"

When Hedi nodded vigorously, the artist went on. "It's not done yet, of course, but—"

A man's voice broke in. "Finished? Let's see." The artist's husband was back, striding across the stage. Noticing Hedi, he said to the woman, "Is this kid bothering you?"

"No, no," she answered hastily. "No, in fact . . . not at all."

"I don't want any distractions, you know. You've got a lot to do between now and the show. Maybe I should stay with you next time."

"You don't really need to. You have your work—"

"We'll see. Now let's look at what you've done."

Hedi retreated to the spot where he'd left his six straw hats. He thought the painting was just fine and should certainly get the man's approval. But there was something about the way the man stood, leaning toward the easel, frowning, that bothered Hedi. It seemed as though he wasn't really looking with admiration or pleasure . . . rather more as though he were buying a horse.

Then the man placed the painting against the restored marble wall at the back of the stage, and started to fold the easel. "It's okay," he said. "They'll like it—it'll sell. Colors need to be a little brighter, but it'll sell quickly enough."

As the two left, Hedi slipped out the other side of the theater, jumping over fallen masonry. He hoped that if the artist came again, her husband would not stay with her. Not just because if the man were there Hedi wouldn't have his protector job, but because he thought the artist looked happy when she was by herself, painting away. She even hummed.

The artist returned alone the next day, midmorning. She did not look surprised to see Hedi waiting; she seemed almost to be expecting him. He wondered how much she would pay him. Or was "tip" the proper term? She and her husband obviously had plenty of money. He wondered whether he should bring the matter up. No, he'd better not say anything, not just yet.

"Many people would envy you," she said, "spending your time in this magnificent site. Do you like it?"

Hedi answered with a shrug. "It's a job. My mother makes the hats, so I sell them. It's okay, I guess. But I get bored. That's why I like to watch you paint."

"And what will you do when you're older?"

That was easier. "I want to get out of here. Go and work at a resort, make some money so I can have a better life. And so my mother won't have to work all the time." The woman was silent, watching him, and he felt impelled to go on. "I want to see the world, the real world like on TV."

"Yes." The woman had her paints and canvas ready for work by now, but she seemed to hesitate. "I suppose a person can feel locked up in almost any place," she said quietly, "even one of sheer beauty."

Hedi felt a daring impulse. "Why don't you paint a picture of *me* today? I'll sit good and still for you." It was just a joke, to make her smile. He didn't expect or even want her to paint him. He wanted only to share a little friendly joke for a moment.

But she turned and looked at him so intently he cringed with embarrassment. He'd annoyed her. Now she'd probably send him away.

When the woman spoke at last, her reply nearly floored Hedi. "All right, I think I will. Go over there and sit. Take the hats, too."

"Hey, I didn't really mean it! I was just—"

"Go and sit down. Any way you like, but don't move. And be quiet."

Meekly he settled himself below a row of columns. Now what had he gotten himself into? This was a fine way to protect! Suppose a big crowd came along—how could he possibly keep them from bothering her? Yet something in the woman's intensity kept him from speaking.

She stood instead of sitting, and soon Hedi noticed that she wasn't using her brushes, applying the paint carefully and precisely as before. Instead she was using a kind of knife, making broad motions with her arm. Frequently she backed away to look at the painting from a little distance, returning to it with quick steps. She seemed excited, humming louder.

Hedi's legs began to tingle, and he itched to move. She'd better pay him extra for this, he thought. But he kept still in spite of the discomfort. At long last the woman spoke to him.

"All right, you can come and see it."

He got up stiffly and went over to look, expecting

another carefully designed view of theater seats and statues, with probably a figure like himself dressed as a Roman, sitting gracefully. But here was a mishmash of paint, and a big twisted figure that didn't look anything like him, just the green of his sweatshirt and pale blue of his jeans, and his dark hair all tousled—purple hair! And the columns—they made shadows on him that looked like prison bars! And the hats were skimming through the air like birds. This was a crazy painting, all right. Crazy.

"You're too close," the artist said.

He stepped back, then a few more steps, and squinted. He looked for a long time. And the longer he looked, the more it seemed to make sense to him. It was real, true, and in a way he couldn't quite understand, disturbing. Wild, like something struggling to break free.

The next moment he heard hurried, firm footsteps.

"I came a little early, Dalenda—" The man stopped short. "Dalenda, what's this? What on earth is *this*?"

She answered quietly. "I wanted to try something different today."

"Oh? Something different? I thought we agreed you'd do only the Echoes series! Because they sell, Dalenda! Because people like them, they *sell*, you know. Who's going to want something like this?"

Suddenly words popped from Hedi's mouth, almost before he knew they were there. "I think it's good. I like it."

The man whirled on him and glared. "What? You—"

From the corner of his eye Hedi saw the woman waver, then abruptly take the canvas from the easel. She approached Hedi and handed him the painting. Clumsy with surprise, he nearly dropped it, catching it just in time.

With a glance at her husband, the artist said, "Someone likes this painting. He shall have it."

"But—but, Dalenda! You can't mean it!" The air seemed to vibrate with his anger. Then the man gave a heavy sigh of exasperation and turned back to Hedi. "Well, kid, you've got an original Dalenda. You'd better appreciate it." As he turned back to the woman, his voice was flat and controlled once more. "I'll be in the car. Don't keep me waiting."

After the man left, Hedi folded the easel and did what he could to help the artist pack up her supplies. He held out the painting, but she shook her head.

"No, it's yours." She looked up at him from beneath the pink bonnet, with a hint of a smile. "And you're right," she said. "It is good."

With a brief thank you, the artist left, lugging all her

gear. Hedi wanted to help, but again she waved him off. Watching her go, recalling the man's cold words, Hedi felt an unexpected anger start to churn inside him. And he knew it wasn't about money.

For a moment as he held the painting, he wondered what he should do with it. Sell it somehow? A painting by this Dalenda artist would probably be worth quite a lot. But he dismissed the idea almost immediately. It wouldn't be right. Besides, the paint was a bit smudged where he'd juggled it.

His eye caught a gleam of something metallic on the ground, and he picked it up. It was the knife she'd been using—she must have dropped it in her hurry to get packed up. Again he looked at the smeared place on the painting. Maybe, he thought, he could fix it a little.

He set the canvas against a column on the marble wall and, holding the knife tentatively, tried to work the still-moist paint. Growing bolder, he gave the knife a dramatic flourish. Then, since no one was around to see, he stepped back, pretending to scrutinize the painting. After a moment he lunged forward to make another tiny dab. Aha . . . just so. Perfect! Hedi, the great painter! So this was what it felt like to be an artist, making the colors and shapes do what you want them to!

56

The woman would come tomorrow, Hedi thought, to look for her knife. Surely she would—she obviously liked working with it. And then maybe he'd ask her to tell him more. What kind of painting she liked most, for instance . . . and how a person could get started being an artist.

Carefully he set the painting in a corner where it would be safe until he was ready to go, then picked up his stack of hats. The afternoon lay before him . . . he'd get busy and try to sell some.

October Sunrise

BY MONICA ARAC DE NYEKO

EVERY DAY THE SUN RISES FROM ITS DEEP-CUPPED sockets in Agoro hills, the place I live, and sets melancholy, beyond the far hills of Mengo, the place my mother lives. That tilting of the sun to deepen the mornings always makes my mind drift away to that day in October, when I was fourteen, the only time my mother ever took me with her to Mengo. It seems like it happened yesterday, so fresh and painful. A memory that hangs about, even when I try to forget it all did happen.

I had no memory of my father. Immediately after my birth I was left with Grandma Esteri, who lived at Agoro hills at the border of Sudan and Uganda, also the place my mother had come to bear me that October 15 sunrise 1990. It is a hilly place with mountains of huge rocks, which seem to tower against each other, like two immense lions. It is the only place I have grown to know-love, the only place I want to know-love.

My memories of my mother are tattooed on my mind. Every December, she comes from Mengo to Agoro, worn out by the eleven-hour journey. Her face is caked in dust and her plaited hair circles her head in big lumps like potato heaps. She is a tall dark woman with much energy and snaky eyes. The week before she will be arriving, she sends word to Grandma Esteri through the Agoro hospital's driver whose car passes through Agoro once every week to deliver medical supplies.

Before that day I was taken to Mengo, Grandma Esteri would send me to wait for her (something I loved doing alone) at the top of the hill. I would see Mama approaching from a distance. She knew I would be there, so she would stand at the foot of the hill, smile a broad smile, and hold out what she had brought for me. Often it was some bright shiny clothes, writing books with paper as white as cottonwool, chocolate, or sweets, which I began looking forward to getting as soon as she left to go back to Mengo, where she lived with my father, the one I had never seen.

One year Mama arrived earlier than we expected. It was October. I had just made fourteen and I hadn't yet written out exams. As soon as she put her luggage down, she headed for Grandma Esteri's hut.

Tiptoeing to the hut, I heard them whispering.

"Don't take the child, Buladina, don't."

Their whispers reminded me of the way the village women looked at me, like they felt sorry for me, as if there was a hidden secret that no one wanted to speak about.

"I have to. She has to get a good education, and this cow-dung school and its house-thatching classes won't help her," Buladina said.

"But. Ummmm . . . " Grandma Esteri seemed doubtful.

"She will be okay, she will, she will. . . . He won't do anything to her."

Buladina was insistent. They argued for what seemed like hours till Grandma Esteri rose up and said, "Do as you wish. Remember a person who doesn't listen goes with human waste to her in-law's home."

The following early morning, Grandma stuffed a few things into her brown traveling bag for me. The night had been heavy with tension, and no one had spoken much. Grandma Esteri did not forget to put in an old teddy bear my mother had brought me on one of her comings. I hated it so far as I can honestly remember, and Grandma Esteri knew. It was like a little monster with all its fuzzy hair. It scared me when I had first seen it, but Grandma tried to make me like it. "It's the only thing he has ever given to you," she often said. The "he" in her words I imagined must be my father, who lived with my mother.

"Here, be a good girl," she stammered now as she handed me the worn-out brown traveling bag with a spoiled zip that left the teddy bear hanging out.

Mama and I traveled from when the cocks crowed to when the skies turned to evening. The big bus that passed through Agoro village to the city was full of chickens cracking and women with small weeping kids. The bus was old. Oh, it was old and rusted, too. I thought we would never reach where we were going, but it rocked on and on till its chest tired of groaning and it stopped like this: *kapuuuuuuum.*

Then Mama, Buladina, held me by the hand as we passed some places with big large women all dressed in small little clothes. It must have been the city, for it looked far better than my Agoro village where Grandma Esteri and me lived. The way Buladina held my hand I had to concentrate more on not tripping than on seeing the city wonders. Tall buildings up to the sky, beggars on the pavements, hawkers on the streets, bright electricity lamps, women in trousers, men with long treated hair . . .

We arrived at Buladina's compound; it had a big house and a small one opposite each other, just like back in Agoro, sleeping room and kitchen in separate buildings, but these were iron roofed and not grass thatched like ours. I was also very excited to see for the first time a full house built of burnt brick, not reeds and mud like the one me and Grandma Esteri slept in.

The place was silent. As we drew nearer, a small light shone from a door opening. Buladina gripped my hand and rushed into the opposite door, where smoke was slipping through into the compound, and inside a small charcoal stove with red-hot coals burning stood at the corner. The room, which was the kitchen, smelled of stale human sweat. A girl seated at a door near the stove stared at Buladina.

"He isn't home," she said.

"Oh, thank God! I was hurrying and breaking my legs with fright." She placed her hand to her chest and turned to me. "Auma Adoch, this is your sister Makareber."

Makareber, who looked a lot older than I was, bent forward. Maybe she hadn't heard what Buladina had just said. She was emotionless. I wanted to move close to her and hold her hand. I had heard so much about her from Grandma Esteri and about home in Mengo, and it was the thought of her that made me think I was not going to miss my friends back at Agoro so much. As I was getting ready to say, "Makareber, my sister," Makareber got a ladle leaning on the paintless wall and stirred the boiling soup in the saucepan. I couldn't believe it. She acted like I wasn't even there, like I smelled of something terrible.

I heard footsteps from outside heading toward the kitchen, and Buladina moved about uneasily. Makareber stirred her soup faster. A tall, huge man stood at the door, peering at us one by one, till his stare settled flat on me. He moved closer a little and pointed to me.

"Who is this?"

"Ummmm . . . It's Auma Adoch."

"Auma Adoch?"

"Yes."

"I thought I told you not to. Come here."

Buladina got up and headed outside. He followed her like a warrior leading his tribe to battle. I got up almost immediately and trailed them from a distance; Makareber did not try to stop me. Buladina and the man did not know I was following. The darkness just swallowed me in her womb.

They headed to the bigger house, directly opposite the kitchen. He banged the door behind her with a roar. It swooped like a strong wind was at its tail but soon settled to a slow, leisurely swing till it stopped midway.

"Why did you bring her?" he thundered.

"Petero, you didn't take any cows to our home; my people do not owe you any bride price," Buladina said. "You have no right to decide whom I bring here."

I stood at the doorway, peering into the dark house through the half-opened door. A small kerosene lamp stood on a metal suitcase.

"Don't talk to me like that, Buladina, don't, don't . . . Buladina, don't . . . " Petero shouted. His voice was ablaze with rage. "I have fed you with food, haven't I? I have covered you with cloth, haven't I? Now don't stand there before me and talk to me like you are the man in this house."

"Auma, get out of there," Makareber called from the kitchen.

"I want to leave. Get out of my way, Petero," Buladina said.

I stood transfixed. I was almost sure what Petero was going to do; he was going to hit her. There was so much awful air around. Then, all of a sudden, there was silence in the house and outside, too. Immediately the thought came to my mind, like that recurrent dream that always poked its way to the depths of my calm sleep, of the monster with the body of a man but whose chest bore a small heart of a grasshopper, hanging. In my dream that man waited for me on the way to the well, and he would dash out and try to grab my little heart and fit it to his, so he could be a full person, but I turned into a bird and flew away; sometimes I was the *olwit* bird, or *openo* bird, but most times I was the *akuru*, the dove—my totem. "I'll get you next time, little girl," the grasshopper-heart man always said. The following morning Grandma Esteri would tell me that my soul had fought with a demon and I had won. "What if I can't fly away next time?" I would ask. She never answered that part. Now I noticed something: My monster in the dream was about the height of Petero.

But this was real. The house had long kissed good-bye to silence, and Petero's voice was raining higher and fiercer each moment as he yelled at Buladina. And it was like he was digging his heavy hands into her small body. He hadn't raised a finger yet, but I felt he was going to thump her head to the brick wall and descend on her like thunder. Then she would fall down and shield her eyes from his venom. His words were now spitting sparks of poison. "Buladina!" he yelled.

I shook and my teeth chattered; I really don't know why.

"Why did you bring her?" he said.

I knew I was the cause of her torment, and I could do nothing for her. Nothing. I felt deceitful, knowing that soon he would beat her up thoroughly and she would be falling down and I, who knew what would happen to her, had done nothing.

"You are not going to beat me again. I am not some kind of mamba snake."

At that moment, I could tell it was the first time she had faced him with boldness. I wanted to be there for her; maybe my presence would help her, who knows? Buladina was standing her ground and telling Petero her mind. It surprised me, although it shouldn't have. I felt the guts in Buladina's tone. Sharp, determined, but scared still.

I had always looked at my living with my grandma as being peculiar but not asked any questions, because it seemed like those questions needed not to be asked. Only children whose mothers did not want them lived with their grandparents in Agoro. And then there were those occasional whispers from some of the villagers. I wanted to ask; I just ended up never doing it. But now I knew my mother's periodic visits were related to this row. There was something very-very terrible-terrible about me.

Petero towered powerfully in front of Buladina. She had the guts to push him out of her way, but she didn't. She had the power to halt him, but she didn't. I knew it. I sensed it. She didn't have to bear his tantrums; she really didn't. But she did. For some reason she had to. Was it for me?

I wanted to stand there and let her feel my presence. I wanted her to know she could do it. For in her voice, I sensed fear, struggle, and pain. She stood, a tall, thin stick of molded sand, her hands on her waist. I could feel them trembling. Trembling. *"You can do it,"* I whispered. *"You can."* Maybe the silent winds of the night would lure my whispers to her ears, maybe, just maybe.

I heard her. "You have no right, you don't . . . that happened and there is nothing I can do about it . . ."

"Don't talk to me like that!"

She opened her mouth to speak . . . and shut up.

Now I could see she was letting go of the courage, every

bit of her nerve was letting go of the fight. Sinister air loomed. Much wasn't being said. I saw her hand on her waist wilt. I was choking, and my head was pounding. She could not lay her hands on his chest and push him out of her way and walk out of his house. She could not, but why?

"Get off me, get off me," she cried suddenly, and tried to push him away as he grabbed her hair and pulled it. She was strong, my mother was strong.

"You are my wife, and I can do whatever I want to you."

Buladina managed to break free and darted through the door; she brushed across me.

Petero ran after her. He stomped the ground with his feet. Darkness swallowed him; it swallowed Buladina. He hadn't noticed me at the door; but as he was trying to run after Buladina he must have seen me, because he came back. Suddenly the darkness let go of him and in the flickering light of the kerosene lamp he stood before me, his eyes smoldering. In that moment I knew he was definitely Petero, my father, whose teddy bear Grandma Esteri insisted I like, whom she did not want Buladina to bring me to, whose pictures she refused to show me. Petero, my father, stood before me.

Daddy stood before me, very close. Buladina, who was

supposed to be hiding somewhere, stood imploring him from a distance. She had come back after he stopped chasing her. "Please leave her alone," she said.

In a moment that seemed eternal, Petero stood before me, his fist clenched. I could feel his fury.

Neighbors filled the compound, voices asking what was going on. Then I saw him lift his hand, higher and higher. "Please, Petero, please," Buladina wailed. In wicked passion he grabbed me by my shoulders and put me under his arm, then dug his heavy hand into my body and thumped my head to the brick wall. I fell down, shielding my eyes from his venom. I heard her again. "You have killed her. Leave my child, leave Auma—"

He grabbed me from the floor and began hitting my head again. Everybody rushed forward. A woman pulled me from under his arm. I could see he wanted to seize my neck and wring it. If I had stayed any longer and the woman hadn't snatched me from his iron hand, I would not be here to tell you this story. Two male neighbors grabbed him, pulling him aside.

"Leave her, whatever she has done, leave her," someone said. Buladina held her hand to her cheeks; torches flashed through the darkness. Makareber got my hand and led me to the kitchen. She put her hand over my swollen forehead and rubbed hard. The pain shifted through my body, but I couldn't let out a sound. I sat, a piece of log, emotionless, blank, frightened.

"Is it painful?" she asked.

"No."

"What!" She rubbed harder.

I could hear voices from outside; Buladina was being led into the kitchen. She was sobbing. She sat by the glowing coals. I looked up to her, seeking an explanation, why had he done this to me? I could tell she was avoiding my eyes. Makareber continued rubbing. "Is she badly hurt?" Buladina asked finally, lifting her head to stare at the corrugated iron sheets and only then at me.

"Is she badly hurt?" she said again.

"But you knew this was going to happen, why ask now? You are lucky there is still air in her lungs and she is alive."

"Is she badly hurt?" my mother said again.

"No," I said. My eyes met with hers, and she swiftly turned away.

"Lie here," Makareber said as she left the kitchen.

It seemed the people were clearing. I opened my mouth to ask but shut it immediately. My head could not think. How would I begin asking . . . Tomorrow, I thought, maybe I will think it over. I crawled over to lie on the papyrus mat, which Makareber spread for me.

Seconds—minutes—hours later, sleep danced across my eyes. The sounds of big drums echoed heavy and somber in the night. They sounded like the drums back in Agoro. Suddenly I heard voices, loud, singing voices. The singing voices rising amid the darkness were deep. I listened to the mingling and crashing of the voices. One particular voice seemed to rise like a smooth and tender lullaby. I moved to listen to the beautiful melody soothing my ears. Then it all went silent, like a passing wind. And it changed; now I was on my way to the dance arena, with the waist beads Grandma Esteri had bought me adorning my waist, and then bang, out of nowhere the grasshopper-heart man appeared, and this time he had changed into a bird and not me. He was flying and going to steal my heart—

A huge rat was nibbling at my toe in my sleep. I moved slightly; I startled him and he ran over a metal tin, making a loud noise. I leaned forward, my eyes torn from dreamland. Beside me in the darkness of the kitchen I noticed a figure. My head felt heavy, a big swollen lump of concealed pain. I looked closer at the figure beside me. "Buladina . . . Buladina," I whispered. "Buladina."

Buladina did not answer me. Instead Makareber, who was beside her, whispered, "He hates you because you are not his child; he thought you were, then he learned you are not. . . . "

I put my head back to sleep that night. Sleep, how it came to my eyes, I will never know. In the morning when I woke, the October sunrise was surprisingly radiant, and a familiar voice was coming from the bigger house. It was shouting at Petero, a tired but tough voice, a voice that had left Agoro some hours after Buladina's and my departure. It had come to follow us. To make right something that should not have happened in the first place, my coming to the city. It was Grandma Esteri's voice.

And she finally said: "I have come to take my child." You should have seen the smile on my face. I wanted that grasshopper-heart man to see it and know he could never get me . . . how could he ever get me, *akuru*, the dove.

Kamau's Finish

BY MUTHONI MUCHEMI

"WOOYAY, PLEASE WITH SUGARCANE JUICE," I SILENTLY pray. "Let me be one of the lucky ones today." Although Kenyatta Primary Academy in Nairobi has almost four hundred students, not many parents have showed up for Sports Day. I don't care about other parents so long as Baba is there for me.

While the headmistress screeches something or other on the squeaky microphone, I scan the group standing on the other side of the track. Baba is not among them. He's tall and big like Meja Rhino the champion wrestler, so you can't miss him.

My team is the Red House, and we're squashed between the Yellow and Blue House teams. Immediately across is the three-step winners' podium. I cross my eyes three times in its direction, shooting lucky *uganga* rays.

But Chris and Daudi pull my T-shirt and break my concentration. I bat their hands away and crouch down. We're sitting on the ground right in front of the track. Mr. Juma, our sports master, let us sit here because we helped him mark the track into lanes with white chalk. Murram dust will fly in our face during the races, but we'll still have the best view.

Suddenly I see a tall figure approaching from a distance and shoot up again. But Baba is half bald, and this man has tight clumps that look like sleeping safari ants scattered about his head.

"Down, Kamau!" barks Mr. Juma.

My race will start in a few minutes. I close my eyes and slowly mouth the secret word. *Ndigidigimazlpixkarumbeta!* Please let Baba be here by the end of this blink. But I open my eyes too soon, way too soon.

Still, I will not lose faith.

Just this morning, I pressed my thumb into the fleshy pad of Baba's thumb. He didn't pull away.

"I have an important business meeting, Kamau, so we'll

just have to see." His dark brown eyes seemed full of heavy thoughts.

I pushed my thumb in harder to drill my way into focus. "Please, Baba . . . "

Mami butted in, "Stop pestering your father. Only thinking about yourself. How selfish can you be?" She is hugely pregnant and can scold until your head vibrates. "Your father has to work. Do you think the money we use to educate you is donated by foreign aid? Maybe you think we can feed on saliva like bacteria, or live on yesterday's skin like fleas? You have no idea about the financial problems—"

Baba coughed. Mami stopped talking, and for a moment they stared at each other. Mami lashed at me again. "What's that mashing thumbs *uganga* anyway?"

My eight-year-old sister, Wanja, laughed, giving us all a good long look at the mushy stuff in her mouth. Neither of my parents said anything about her bad manners. She had just shown them her report card and, as vomit usual, she was first in her class. Of course, they then asked for mine, and I had to dig it out of the bottom of my bag.

"'Kamau needs to concentrate. He is easily distracted . . .'" Mami had waved the report at Baba. "Didn't I tell you that all this boy does night and day is dream? If they tested a subject called dreaming, Kamau's grades would burst through the ceiling and pierce the cover of the sky!"

Baba had nodded his head in Mami's direction. Did he agree with Mami?

"Kamau's head is full of nonsense!" She'd prodded my head. I let it bob up and down like a rubber ball on a string. "He needs to knuckle down. I want him to succeed. Achievement is what matters. Maybe he dreams he'll be the next president of this country. President Kamau? Heh! Kamau, get serious. Even future kings need to work."

It was no use telling her I try.

My friend Chris once told me his mother said babies in the belly kick. So I squinted and sent mega-*uganga* rays to the baby in Mami's belly to make its legs stronger. She stopped talking and placed a hand over her side.

Maybe my *uganga* rays were too strong.

I held my breath in awe of my powers, but nothing else happened.

Then Njau, my four-year-old brother, had piped up in his high voice, "Baba said effort is what matters."

Baba rumbled, "And problems help us grow."

Mami had scrunched her face as though a mountain of

firewood pressed her head and waddled off to pack my special energy lunch—sweet potato slices, *maziwa lala,* boiled egg, two carrots, and an orange.

I bite into the pad of my thumb. It's tingling. *Ndigidigimazlpixkarumbeta!*

"Sit down, Kamau, how many times do I have to tell you?" Mr. Juma's voice rises up and whips me back down.

I glance over at the Yellows and silently chant, "Yellow, yellow, dirty fellow," when my eyes lock with Kip's. He points his index finger and cocks his thumb at me. I duck the imaginary bullet, but he's laughing, trading high-fives with his mates, and doesn't notice. Kip is ten, a year younger than most of my class, and usually the fastest. But twice during practice runs this term, I beat him. He spat at me and sulked off. Everyone else clapped me on the back, even Mr. Juma.

When I told Baba, he said, "Well done, son," and "Good for you."

Now if only Baba would get here, I'd show him how I did it. I'd prove to him that I'm not just a hopeless dreamer.

Our 800-meter race is announced over the screechy microphone. I stare desperately at the parents' side of the track as we file to the starting block. He isn't there.

Three runners from each team stand at attention. Mr. Juma calls for silence.

"Good luck," says Chris in a hoarse voice.

"Same to you," I whisper as we crouch down in starting position.

"On your marks!"

Daudi is in the farthest lane. His lips are moving in silent prayer. Kip calls him *mkiha*, the last carriage of a train. Of course, Kip sees himself as the engine, the one that always gets to its destination first.

I look past Daudi. No sign of Baba, only other parents jostling to get a better view of their sons at the starting line.

Mami said I was selfish to need Baba here today, but I so want to prove to him and Mami that I can be a winner. If he comes just this once, I'll never ask him again.

"Get set!"

I look down at my hands splayed on the ground and feel such a sharp tingling in my thumb that I glance up.

And there he is! My thumb never lies. There is Baba, pushing his way through the throng of parents along the track. There is no mistaking that huge shining head floating above the rest, hurrying in my direction.

Boom! The gun goes off.

I want to burst with happiness. But a blur of bodies has already bolted forward. They have a head start.

I have to concentrate on the race instead of thinking about the miracle of Baba being here. I glue my eyes on the nearest runner, a blue T-shirt. I concentrate on catching up with him. I run like Ananse the hungry hare on his way to Mr. Elephant's feast. I overtake him.

Concentration, concentration, concentration now begins. To that beat, I run faster. I run in long hard strides that bounce off the ground and pull on the backs of my thighs. My legs feel strong. I set my sights on a yellow back. A surge of warmth floods my body as I overtake him.

I can tell it's Daudi directly in front of me, because he runs with his head facing the sky. He's already slowing. I pound past him with my eyes locked on Kip's yellow shirt.

He's in a cluster, but I know Kip always goes for the flashy sprint finish. I have to catch up with him now if I'm to have a chance. Concentration, concentration, concentration now begins.

Amid all the crowd noises, I think I hear Baba yell, "Run, son!"

A new energy tingles from my feet, up along my legs,

loosens my hips, and expands my chest. I tear past Chris, who is panting like a horse. *Uganga* magic is with me!

The cluster is breaking up. Kip is racing ahead. My heart hammers in my ribs. I open my mouth wider to take in more air. I'm catching up. I'm in the dispersing cluster. I overtake one, two, three boys.

I'm flying, my feet almost slapping my bottom, half a step behind Kip.

When I win this race, Mami will never scold me again. When I win this race, Wanja will swallow her snickering. Best of all, Baba will look in my eyes to congratulate me. Baba will finally see me.

Everything feels slow motion. The noise, the people, and the track float away into the great *uganga*-land of dreams. I hear only distant echoes. "Win, win, win!"

I'm neck and neck with Kip, matching him stride for stride. He leans in my direction as though to draw strength from me. The finish-line ribbon flutters red maybe fifty meters ahead.

I'm going to win! I'm going to win! My teammates will carry me on their shoulders, shouting, "Hero! Hero!" When I climb the winner's podium to collect my medal, I won't even punch the air or do a show-off dance. Baba will already know I'm a hero. Baba will—

An unexpected shove jolts me out of my dream and back to the moment. Then I'm wobbling, fighting for control. I fall.

Unbelievable!

I swallow the grit on my tongue and shake my head to clear the ringing in my ears. I feel confused. Not quite on this earth. My hands are grazed with white track chalk mixed with brown soil and smudges of blood. I shape them into fists and press hard to force the pain away. A blue shirt whizzes by, kicking dust in my face.

While I was in my dream, Kip must have pushed me with his elbow. Mami would be proud of a son like Kip, who knows winning is what matters.

Legs zoom past me in a whir of hot air and dust. I glance toward the side of the track. The crowd probably thinks Kip and I touched accidentally.

A cheer goes up and I realize Kip must have crossed the red ribbon. Kip has won my race. No. Kip has stolen my race.

I want to call to Baba that I should have won. Will he believe that Kip tripped me?

Most of the runners are finishing. Daudi rushes past me, his tongue lolling out of his mouth, probably elated not to be the *mkiha* for once.

I look back and see Baba's shiny face. He is running alongside the track, gesturing wildly—up, up, up—pointing to the finish line. But how will getting up help me? I'll pretend my leg is broken. I'll give a dramatic cry for help. I'll—

I become aware of the noise, the cheering. They're chanting my name. "KA-MA-UU! KA-MA-UU! KA-MA-UU!" They're shouting for me to finish. I feel like shouting back, "Whatever for? All I'm good for is dreaming."

Then I notice their eyes are not on me, but on my lumbering Baba, who has crossed onto the track behind me. He is wearing a black suit and shiny lizard shoes he bought donkey years ago that usually make me cringe.

My ears buzz, but I think I hear him shout, "Run, son! Get up and run!"

Uncertain, I scramble up and gape at Baba. Sweat streams down his face, and he holds a hand over his chest. Is he having a heart attack?

He can't be. His eyes are shining. I can see every tooth in his mouth.

Baba is beaming!

So I wipe my nose with my wrist and laugh through the tears. It sounds like I am crying. But Baba is beaming.

I keep my eyes on him and trot sheepishly alongside to the finish. So much noise, so many people crowding the finish area. Mr. Juma is probably shouting for order.

But I only have ears for Baba.

AMERICANS IN AFRICA

Into the Maghreb

BY LINDSEY CLARK

My mom knows a country far away,

bordering the Great Desert,

separated from the rest of its continent by sand.

"You will see my history," she whispers,

her smile a promise

as our plane soars high above the Atlantic.

Casablanca. Door to Morocco.

Women walk arm in arm.

Men hold hands.

Banana juice stains café tables that

spill onto sidewalks.

Minarets of mosques tower,

and I am small and far from home.

"*Vous etes touristes ici en Maroc?*"

asks the staring driver.

hna mashi franzawiyat, we are not French,

my mother replies with the look of remembering.

On the train, greenbrown fields and station stops—
Rabat, Sidi Slimane, Meknès, Fès—
fly by
but remain as memory.
Bright sun tightens my skin,
and we walk into the past
where power lines end,
cars become horses,
and a dirt path brings us to a village in the hills.

Our arrival is an explosion.
Children in bright mismatched clothing
holler and hide behind fathers who
shake my mother's hand;
women kiss her cheeks endlessly while
I hang back, watching.
Fatima khootee, Fatima my sister,
my mom weeps happily
when a woman wearing her eyes
pushes through the crowd to her arms.

ajee, Fatima beckons us
into her whitewashed mud kitchen,
where the women are in command.
Dark eyes lined in kohl,
open smiles spattered with empty tooth sockets,
hair wrapped loosely in soft scarves,
and the earthy smell of henna-stained hands.
The women move to the rhythm
of metal pot drums,
rotating their hips in a playful dance
the men will never see.

In a corner the pressure cooker hisses.
Soon potatoes, lentils, peppers, fava beans,
pour onto the family plate.
Koolee, koolee, koolee! Eat, eat, eat!
A dozen bodies in a circle on sheepskin mats,
a dozen brown hands sweep up vegetables
with chunks of homemade flatbread
still warm from the fire.

Through the bullhorn on the mosque across the stream
rises up a mournful scratchy voice:
Allah akbar, God is great.
On mats in the next room
the men bow, submitting to Islam
as the women submit to them
and the family submits to the pattern of each day.

Darkness falls so gradually
I don't notice until my hand reaches
for a light switch that isn't there.
Sheep trample down from the hills
through the kitchen to the manger.
Chickens are locked into the bathroom for the night,
and donkeys bray in the dimming light.

The final flurry
is the laying down of blankets
across the floor
and the laying down of our bodies
across the room.

Fatima nods a silent message,

and my cousin's small cool hand slips into mine.

Amina gently leads me from my mother's side

and pulls me down

into a sandwich of sleepy Moroccan sisters.

Eyes close, limbs shift, hushed whispers subside,

and Fatima's warm voice reaches out:

marhaba andkoom, bnaatee merikaniyat,

marhababikoom . . .

Welcome home, my American daughters, welcome.

And I know a country

no longer far away

but part of me.

Our Song

BY ANGELA JOHNSON

I'VE ALWAYS HEARD THE SONG. I CAN'T EVER REMEMBER a time when the song didn't come real soft and sweet out of my great-great-grandma, or Ole Ma, as we all call her.

She always sings it for me and me only. She says it's an old song from Senegal about a girl who lived a long time ago. She only sings it in her village language though.

So I sit and listen and dream the song is about me, and I sure do like that I'm named after her.

She has black-and-white pictures of people from her village in Senegal, Africa, all over her room. There are rugs on her floor she says her sister from Africa sent her, baskets and rugs from back home.

Ole Ma says on days when the wind blows she thinks that she can imagine all the food smells and wood smoke from her village.

She says it gets carried on the breeze.

Anyway, Ole Ma's room is the only one in the house where I can play basketball. She let me put a net on the back of her closet door. She even has shoot-outs with me sometimes. Ole Ma is my biggest fan. Nobody else at home understands me and my moods except her.

Ole Ma says, "Child, will you be playing that round-ball game on the television one day like those other girls?"

And that is when I sit down by her feet. Ole Ma has big feet like me. I always tickle them and make her laugh.

She says that her big feet are what helped her get a husband. Even though she wasn't looking for one, just running around her village in Senegal with her friends when all of a sudden a boy who would turn out to be great-great-grandaddy fell at her feet. He tripped over her feet.

She was the same age as I am now. Ten.

They would be friends for ten years, then marry.

But Ole Ma hardly ever talks about that kind of stuff to me; all she wants me to do is get good grades and one day play basketball on television.

She says that boys are different now, and I don't understand that. They all seem the same to me when I beat them at basketball or outrun them.

Ole Ma says that everything was different in her village when she was young. I always wonder what it was like, but even though she tells some stories, she ends each one by saying, "But all that's not important, my girl, how is school and everything that moves around you?"

The first time she said that I turned around 'cause I thought she saw something.

I said, "You see something, Ole Ma?"

Ole Ma just laughed and reached down from her old chair and squeezed my face. Then she sang the song that she says her Ole Ma taught her.

In all the times Ole Ma has sung the song to me, which was probably from the time I was a real little baby and she'd just moved in with us, I'd never thought about learning the song.

All the words are in another language that I don't understand. But I like the words, whatever they are.

Ole Ma sang the song for me the time my arm got

broken after I tried to make a jump shot on a junior high boy who said girls couldn't play real basketball.

I made the shot, though.

She sang the song for me when I fell off the roof after my best friends, Buddy and Charlotte, bet each other they could land in my mom's lavender bushes.

Charlotte said, "We're not even asking you, Josie, 'cause we already know you'll do it."

The next thing any of us knew, I was in the lavender, then in the backseat of my brother Jamal's car, then in the hospital with Charlotte and Buddy yelling at each other that it wasn't like they included me in the bet or anything.

The nurses all knew me, and when they called me by name, Jamal just put his head in his hands and stayed that way for a while.

Momma says Ole Ma was delicate when she was my age and probably doesn't understand the trouble I get in. She says I should be more like Ole Ma was.

But all that's not important 'cause now Ole Ma is laughing as I tickle her feet and lean against her as she starts to sing her song. The wind blows through her curtains and I can smell my momma's flowers in the yard.

I fall asleep to the sound of Ole Ma's song.

Just like that.

. . .

Ole Ma says that it has been a long time coming, but now is the time. We are going back to where she grew up in Senegal.

She said it at the dinner table last night, and I was the only one there who was surprised.

My sister, Nita, kept moving her head to whatever was on her Walkman. Jamal smiled. Momma and Daddy looked across the table at me and then smiled down at the other end at Ole Ma.

Even though I had a mouth full of food I still spoke. "When?"

Mama laughed. "We'll be leaving around your winter break in a couple of months."

I was happy. "Africa is so far away I'll probably need to miss a whole lot of school—right? I mean, we don't just want to go for a couple of days, then come right home, do we?"

Daddy says, "I don't think two weeks is such a short time by plane. And anyway, we'll make sure you don't miss any school, Josie. We all know how much that would upset you."

Daddy is always trying to be funny, but it doesn't matter. I will finally see where my Ole Ma is from. I get to see the place her husband fell over her big feet and the places she ran around with her friends. I am going to Africa.

I run around the village my Ole Ma grew up in.

I run around the village with my cousins. Cousins that I sort of knew I had, cousins that Ole Ma talked about around the table and in her chair before she went to sleep at night. But they were always dream cousins to me.

These are the real cousins.

They are the cousins that show me the secret places in the village. They show me where they go when they want to hide from the adults. They show me the field that they all play soccer in. They also show me (when we stand on top of my cousin Leo's house) where they bag groundnuts (peanuts) to ship off to everywhere in the world.

There are mountains and mountains of them as we stand on the roof and look off into the blue sky.

It's the end of December and it's warm enough in my Ole Ma's village to be wearing a tank top and shorts. I am. It's warm enough to be standing outside with no shoes, even though Momma yells at me about that and makes me put a hat on my head.

None of the other kids are wearing hats.

And I want to run barefoot like them.

• • •

Even though my cousins can't speak much English, they smile and pat me on the back when I try to speak some French; 'cause they can speak it and I took it when I was in second grade. But mostly we just point or laugh.

My cousin Leo's village is outside a city called Dakar. Tomorrow we are all going there for market day. I can't wait. Leo talks about the food and all the traders and the excitement of the market. It won't be like the grocery stores back home.

I wake up beside Leo and his little sisters Doni and Victoria on the covered mats in the backyard. Sleeping outside in December! The sky is just starting to turn pink when I hear our song. Ole Ma's song is being hummed by somebody I can't see, and it isn't Ole Ma.

So I go looking.

First I should tell how Ole Ma has done nothing but smile and be surrounded by people who visit our cousins' little house and sit and talk and talk way into the night.

She smiles at me when I run past her with a soccer ball or kneel beside her when we eat our dinner, at least I call it dinner.

Sometimes some of the older village women stop me

when I'm running past with my cousins and call me Little Goat. I just smile 'cause they all seem to know me as Ole Ma's great-great-grandchild.

I'm used to it now like I'm used to carrying a soccer ball everywhere I go. And I'm getting used to the dry desert village and people who speak a different language and kind of look like me.

At home when I watched shows on television and they would show Senegal I'd always search for a tall girl who looked just like me. Now I see a lot of people who look like me and are related.

Anyway, Ole Ma is so happy to be back in her village. To be back home.

On this early morning, though, even before the chickens start to move again, I hear Ole Ma's song.

When I start walking down the center of the road I don't think much about it. Nobody is out yet and I pretty much know every place. But I don't think I remember the little hut at the end of the village road.

Someone is up besides me. She comes out of the mist that circles the little hut. She dances around, then runs around. She starts talking to people I can't see in the hut, then runs ahead of me.

"Hey, wait for me," I call.

I do know that when I look at Ole Ma from now on I will see Africa. I will know where we all come from.

But most important, I will know who Ole Ma really was when I hear our song, and learn in the old way to sing it one day to my great-great-granddaughter. So one day she'll say she's always heard the song and can't remember a time when it didn't come soft and sweet from her great-great-grandma.

The Homecoming

BY MARETHA MAARTENS

"JUST ASK," LINCOLN'S FATHER SAID. HE SMELLED OF toothpaste and aftershave. "The kids won't mind you asking them to explain things. Just try not to be so utterly negative." He was fixing up the old-fashioned navy blue school tie that Lincoln was now compelled to wear.

Another endless day at school in South Africa lay ahead of Lincoln. Never in the history of mankind had the days and the hours been so long and hot. "From day three on," his dad had said last week, "you will be okay. Remember that survival camp you attended at the Shenandoah National Park? You thought you'd never make it. From day three on, however, you were like a cat in a fishery. Mark my words, Lincoln: You are at the turning point."

You bet. His fifth day at Afrikaans Senior Primary loomed ahead and here he was, feeling as awful as ever. It was blue Monday, and he was like the *fish* in that fishery.

"I hear them laughing behind my back all the time, Dad," said Lincoln. "Yesterday on the playground one guy wanted to know why you got it into your head to return to Africa after living in the States for fifteen years. Then lots of others closed in on me. They breathed on me and pushed me and one of them whispered something about you being a black man from Africa and Mom—"

"—being an African American." Lincoln's school tie done, his father reached for his coffee. He stirred it as if sugar took longer to dissolve in Africa than in America. "That's okay with me. They'll get over it. You'll be okay, too."

Flippit, Lincoln thought. I'm not negative, Dad. Africa is just such an odd planet.

He had to laugh at himself. *Flippit* seemed to be one of the most frequently used words on South African school grounds. He was picking up new words without even realizing it.

He took his satchel and opened the creaky front door of the brick house his parents had rented. On the far side of the veranda lay the overgrown garden with its unpruned peach, quince, and kumquat trees. He could hear the voices, the whistles, the laughter, and the calls of children on their way to school.

"You haven't eaten much of your breakfast," his mother said behind him. "And I didn't hear any good-byes, either."

Lincoln sighed. "I was just *looking*, Mom." He smiled a wobbly smile. "As you always say, 'Look before you leap, Lincoln.'"

She reached out and ruffled his hair. Her eyes were kind but worried. "You'll be okay, Lincoln. That boy who invited you to spend this Friday afternoon at his place sounds like a great kid. What's his name again?"

"Manfred April," said Lincoln. "See you, Mom. . . . Bye, Dad. . . . " He didn't mention that Manfred had suggested making it the whole weekend.

"Your sandwiches," said his mother, handing him his lunch box.

Babying him again. But this Monday morning was blue enough. "Thanks, Mom." He walked down the garden path, opened the front gate, and braced himself. Okay, the mountains surrounding the town of Oudtshoorn were impressive. He knew it would be exciting to visit the Cango Caves and some of the ostrich farms in the district. But it was ghastly to feel like an alien.

Lincoln hated being stared at. He hated being interrogated about life in the U.S.A., about his parents' return to South Africa, about American football and the Winter Olympics, about junk food and video games and Halloween. He hated the smell of Marmite, the black sandwich spread that everybody in South Africa seemed to love. He hated the ostrich *biltong* that everybody wanted him to taste. And he hated the language everybody spoke and in which they made fun of him.

But for some reason everybody cycling past him, everybody in front of him, and everybody behind him seemed to know his name:

"Hi, Lincoln!"

"Howzit, Lincoln?"

"Sports Day tomorrow, Lincoln!"

How he missed Washington! How he missed his noisy friends, his top-rated school with its leafy playground, the wide boulevards, the Japanese cherry trees along the Tidal Basin, the safe, air-conditioned subway cars of the Washington Metro . . . everything that used to be part of his life!

• • •

"English with Miss van der Riet!" said Manfred April, lifting the top of the school desk he shared with Lincoln, ducking behind it, and biting noisily into a huge yellow peach. "Uggggh. I hate English with Miss van der Riet." He took a second grinding bite, keeping a watchful eye on the open classroom door. "I liked the student who stood in for her, didn't you? She was fun. But count on Miss van der Riet. Not even an operation will keep her in hospital. She'll drag herself to Afrikaans Senior Primary just to get her claws into us. She is . . . as dangerous as they come."

"Really?" whispered Lincoln.

"Wait and see," said Manfred, hastily putting the remainder of the peach back into the pocket of his frayed school trousers.

Miss van der Riet wore dusty glasses. She sported a blob of dry toothpaste on the lapel of her pink summer jacket, and even at this early hour, the sweat was streaming down her face. While she was writing on the blackboard Lincoln had the uneasy feeling that she was going to corner him. He was right. She had somehow sensed that he was a bookworm, a book snake, a book anaconda. When she turned around, she said, "Now, Lincoln, let's start with you. What have you been reading lately? And do you have any positive or negative views on any of those books?"

Lincoln could feel his classmates' stares. From the corner of his eye he saw Manfred giving him a tiny, secretive thumbs-up sign, but that didn't help.

"I—I like *Lord of the Rings*, ma'am," he mumbled.

Miss van der Riet's eyes brightened. She went on and on about Frodo and Gandalf and Gollum: "So what do you think of Gollum, Lincoln? Gollum is oddly fascinating, isn't he? Only a great author like Tolkien could have created a creature like that."

Lincoln nodded nervously. She was flashing her kindly killer smile at him. "Would you mind telling the class about Gollum, Lincoln?"

Miss van der Riet was genuinely psychic to put her finger on his fascination with Gollum, and he fell into her trap, boots and all:

"He . . . Gollum lived in a hole at first," Lincoln said. "And later on he met up with Frodo. That's where the story becomes really interesting. I think everybody should see *The Two Towers*, which is part two of the film version of the book. Gollum is . . . "

They were poking one another in the ribs, of course. He would have done the same. He swallowed the last part of the sentence. He was perspiring like Miss van der Riet.

He had gone hopelessly overboard. If only he could become the Invisible Boy from the U.S.A.

"Teacher's pet!" somebody whispered behind his back. But Miss van der Riet turned her head ever so slowly, and the whispering stopped.

I *have* to keep my big mouth shut, Lincoln thought miserably. Gollum has gotten me into a mess.

But Manfred April did not share his feelings. During break Manfred asked: "What kind of creature is a gollum?"

"A miserable creature," Lincoln said, feeling more miserable than Gollum himself. "He possessed the One Ring for a while."

Manfred was definitely not the reading type. Lincoln could have guessed that Manfred would be a bad speller; that he would be easily distracted and would fool around in class. Nothing like his friends in Washington, D.C. No going to the library together, no computer games, no skateboard riding.

He again had the almost familiar sinking feeling about a whole weekend at Manfred's place. Perhaps they should have kept to one afternoon. Perhaps they still should.

"You have read *Lord of the Rings*, haven't you?" Lincoln asked politely.

"I haven't seen anybody borrowing that book from the school library," replied Manfred. "I suppose they haven't got it there. My English is anyhow much too *vrot* for a book like that!"

He grinned bashfully. "So you won't believe this, but I would like to read the book, just to find out more about that old wizard and this gollum creature. The goody two-shoes *oke* doesn't tickle me so much. It's a pity that movie about the towers won't come to Oudtshoorn."

Lincoln was taken aback. Frodo was no goody-goody. He did not argue with Manfred, though. He might have been mistaken, but for one millionth of a second he had seen something like real longing in Manfred's eyes. So he patiently described Gollum to him: how mummylike and slimy and shriveled he was.

Manfred grinned again. "This Gollum creature reminds me of moles and snails and leeches."

"Leeches?" Weren't those something from the . . . Middle Ages?

"You won't know leeches," Manfred said cheerfully. "It's a worm with a sucker at each end of its body. It feeds on the blood of animals and babies. It clings like mad. When I heard that creature's name I thought to myself: This one must surely be slimy and leechlike."

114

"That is what Gollum looked like," Lincoln said rather helplessly. "He looked exactly like a leech. But in the movie he has . . . marblelike eyes."

"Sports Day tomorrow, Lincoln!" his schoolmates had sung out to him yesterday. And Sports Day it was. He had not even prayed for a miracle like a hailstorm, a hurricane, or a tornado.

Lincoln was bulldozed to the sports field. He fervently hoped that Manfred would pop up from somewhere. He did not know what to expect. Even his classmates looked totally different in shorts and sleeveless tops and T-shirts. Luckily Manfred appeared from nowhere, his grin as wide as ever, once again stumbling and bumbling across the language barrier: "Howzit, Lincoln? *Jislaaik*, that's a nice pair of tackles on your feet. You know we are allowed to run *kaalvoet*, don't you?" Nobody had warned Lincoln that he would have to master the South African version of English that was so heavily spiced with weird Afrikaans words.

Manfred was happy and in control. "Let's find a spot where we can leave our *kos* till after the race. *Pasop*—there are ants over there. Man, you've got a *windgat* tracksuit! You'll be *lekker* hot and bothered by nine o'clock!"

If it weren't for Manfred, thought Lincoln, I would take

refuge in one of the caves in the Outeniqua Mountains towering above the town.

The kids in the pavilion seats were singing and chanting, waving red, green, and yellow flags, and roaring the battle cries of the various teams. Miss van der Riet, her nose and parts of her glasses smeared with blue sunblock, shuffled past him in the most ridiculous outfit he had ever seen.

"Good morning, Lincoln," she said over her shoulder. "Your first school athletics event in Africa!"

"She's going to make you do an oral on this," muttered Manfred darkly. "But try not to think about that today. Let's get to the pavilion. Check there: Lila is going to run the hundred meters."

"Lila?"

"My sister. She's like a flash of lightning. She's the only one who can catch that snake of mine when he is in a playful mood."

Halfway up the pavilion, Lincoln stopped in his tracks.

"Did you say . . . snake?"

"Of course," said Manfred. "He is a *skaapsteker* and his name is Das."

"What does that mean?"

"Das? *Skaapsteker?* Okay. Das means . . . well, it means . . . tie. Like bow tie, black tie, school tie, principal's tie."

Manfred April mimicked the school principal tugging at his wildly patterned tie. "You should see the symmetrical patterns on his skin." He climbed over some of their class-mates' knees, gesticulating that Lincoln should do the same and talking nonstop at the top of his voice. "Those patterns are just unbelievable. As for *skaapsteker . . . flippit . . .* that's difficult to explain in English. It means that this is a species that bites sheep."

"Are *skaapsteker* snakes aggressive, then?" Lincoln screamed. He had to scream; the singing and roaring around them was deafening.

"Some of the white *okes* . . . " Manfred looked over his shoulder and grinned mischievously. "Some of the white *okes* say *skaapstekers* are nasty and prone to biting. That's pure nonsense. Mine is a fat glutton, let me tell you. That snake of mine puts away mice and lizards by the dozen. He loves frogs, but we get so little rain here that snakes forget what frogs look like. Mind you, the white *okes* will try to spin you a yarn."

Oke. Another odd word. More than once Lincoln had heard Manfred scolding some of the younger kids who often giggled behind their backs—"Give this *oke* a break, okay?" His high-pitched rebuke usually worked. Lincoln had not been able to figure out why.

"There's Lila," said Manfred proudly. "In the third lane. She's just dying to get going."

I hope Lila sticks to us during the weekend, thought Lincoln. Like a leech. Or like a flash of lighting, striking between us and that *skaapsteker* snake.

Friday afternoon. He had survived nine days of school at Afrikaans Senior Primary. Or nine centuries.

Manfred was spitting like a champion. The spittle hit a brown pebble, and he flexed his biceps triumphantly. "Check that, Lincoln. Spot on." Lincoln was dragging himself along in the shimmering heat. Manfred, however, was walking lightly, like a long-distance hiker, the plastic supermarket bag with his schoolbooks slung over his shoulder.

"It's not forever," Mom had said. "You're going to have fun. A weekend of cave crawling, hill hiking, and donkey-cart riding sounds marvelous to me. It's something different."

You bet. The fun has started. Lincoln could hear some of his new classmates behind them. Manfred seemed unperturbed, but Lincoln could lay his head on a block that they were saying things about him: *Oke, oke.* Teacher's new pet . . . ha-ha. Several of them were throwing stones at the telephone poles lining the highway. Every time he heard the dull thud of a stone hitting a wooden pole, Lincoln bit his lip.

He got some satisfaction out of thinking that his mother would be horrified if she could see him walking on the shoulder of the highway, but this was Oudtshoorn, South Africa. The lumbering 1976 school bus had broken down again. Everybody had to walk home, and nobody cared.

"What should I do if Manfred brings that snake into the bedroom?" he had asked his father the previous evening. His timing was bad, he knew, but his dad nevertheless had his famous I'll-always-stand-by-you look on his face. Poor Dad was carrying the whole world on his shoulders, the world being Mom and Lincoln, Gusto the tomcat, and Prof, Dad's beloved African Gray parrot, who had caused pandemonium at the Johannesburg International Airport.

Dad had sighed one of his quiet sighs and assured him that *skaapsteker* snakes would not bite humans, even when provoked. "But never trust an ostrich," his father had added. "There are only two things you can do when an ostrich chases and attacks you. Get hold of a forked stick. Poke it at the base of his neck. You'll be able to keep the old bird at a distance that way. It won't be able to kick at you. Ostriches are rather stupid, after all. I grew up on an ostrich farm. I know."

Lincoln had stared at his father. His face was leaner and livelier than in Washington.

"A second alternative," his father was saying, "would be to fall flat on the ground and to lie with your face in the sand, making a fortress wall around your face with your arms. An attacking ostrich may decide to sit on you and peck at you the moment you move. So don't. It will peck at the buttons on your clothes but also at your eyes, should you move."

"Did that ever happen to you, Dad?"

"Of course! I once went home minus the buckle of my belt. A huge male ripped it off and swallowed it! As for those *skaapsteker* snakes—"

"Oh, come on, William!" Lincoln's mother had laughed. "The boy has more than enough to handle and to adapt to. So have I."

"A peach for your thoughts." Manfred jerked a yellow clingstone peach out of his pocket and offered it to Lincoln. He was smaller than Lincoln, scrawny and agile like an athlete or a dancer. But rocklike, Lincoln thought. Solid and different, right from day one.

They were crossing a road with lots of potholes and a surface of boiling asphalt.

Lincoln bit into the peach. It tasted like something that had dropped from heaven. He ate hungrily and ended up with the peach pit in his mouth.

"I've been thinking about how shockingly hot it is here for February," Lincoln mumbled. The peach pit made him sound dumb. He spat it out, very Africa–ish.

"Yes, here February is hot and plain hard work," Manfred said. "Most people are picking and packing peaches. We've now got stupid laws prohibiting child labor, but I'm trying to worm my way into the orchards. Last year I earned a lot of money at picking and packing. I bought my great-grandfather a good secondhand coat and woolen socks. We will be having a cake sale at our church; my mum is responsible for the *koeksisters*. Which means more hard work. At half past ten last night I was still packing *koeksisters*. I was so sticky and sugary that I could have been mistaken for a flytrap."

Lincoln's father had told him about this number-one treat of his childhood. "A *koeksister*," his father had said dreamily, "is a syrupy doughnut, translucent and crisp. My mother used to cut and plait the dough; *koeksisters* resemble small plaits."

121

"My mum is the *koeksister* queen of the town," Manfred was saying. "Our claim to fame."

Lincoln grabbed his wrist. "There's something in the shrub over there. Not a bird. It has four legs."

"That is a rock dassie." Manfred spat on the ground. "There's another one. Look at the big one: That's the tribal chief. It is easy to identify the males: When you see incisor teeth sticking out from behind a rock dassie's upper lip, you are spotting a male."

"Are they dangerous?" Lincoln asked. "Will they attack humans?"

"Of course not." Manfred laughed. "They're all over the place. They feed on leaves and grass. There are poisonous plants that sheep and goats won't touch. These rock dassies eat anything, just like Das. I do hope that that snake of mine will be around when we get home."

Lincoln kept a straight face. There was but one alternative: to turn back and lose his only friend.

"From here on we have to watch out for puff adders," said Manfred. "Now *those* snakes are really poisonous. But we have been crawling through this fence for ages." He held the barbed wire down with his bare foot, and Lincoln scraped through.

The terrain was becoming rougher; they were leaving

the asphalt road behind. By now, Lincoln's right shoe was pinching him and his left shoe was chafing his heel to blisters.

One of the kids traipsing behind them sneezed. They had crawled through the fence too. Lincoln could feel the invisible cloud of germs on the back of his neck.

Manfred turned around. "Skedaddle, okay?" he said to the mob at their heels. "Scoot off." Some of the boys made faces at Manfred, but to Lincoln's surprise the pack broke up to take other footpaths through the veld and over the low, rocky hills.

"How did you do that?" Lincoln asked.

"Kickboxing," said Manfred. "Our preacher's son teaches me all the kicks. These *okes* know I get my kicks from kicks."

Lincoln laughed. The most unlikely *oke* in the school had become his friend and guardian. Not once had this guy with his black messed-up hair, his dusty kneecaps, his bitten-off fingernails, and cracked heels left him hanging.

"There's our place," Manfred said with a wave. "I hope my great-dad is still up. He takes a nap sometimes, especially when it is as hot as it is today."

He grinned. "He doesn't like speaking English, not even to be polite. But make no mistake: He understands every word. When he was much younger he worked for an English-speaking farmer who often whipped him. My great-granddad was his goatherd. Goats look strong and hardy, but they die like flies in wintertime. They wander off and go grazing in the mountains and in other stupid places. My great-granddad couldn't be everywhere to get them all into the *kraal*. So each winter some of them froze to death. And then my great-granddad was given thrashing after thrashing."

Lincoln stared at Manfred. He wanted to say the right thing, but he was speechless.

"So expect anything," said Manfred happily.

Gollum! Lincoln thought when his eyes had become used to the semidarkness of the kitchen. This is unreal. The real Gollum is sitting over there in the corner.

Manfred's great-grandfather was so small and transparent and skeletonlike that he was almost invisible. His head was a skull with ancient skin draped over it. His hands were like claws; his shoulders were those of a six-year-old.

But his eyes were inquisitive and bright.

"I'm glad you are up, Great-Daddy," Manfred was saying. "Let me introduce you to the boy from Washington. His name is Lincoln Paulsen; his daddy grew up in this part of the country. His mom is a Yankee, though."

"Speak Afrikaans, son," the old man said, eyeing Lincoln.

Manfred shrugged and translated. A high-pitched, melodic medley of quaint sounds filled the room. Lincoln felt the almost irresistible urge to try to pronounce the word daddy in the way Manfred did. He knew how he'd go about it. First he would smile his broadest smile, his yippee!-we-are-returning-to-the-States smile. Without wiping the smile off his face, he would form the word daddy right at the tip of his tongue, making the *a* sound like the vowels in hair. The word that he had used and known for thirteen years would be converted into something different, something uniquely African.

But Manfred was doing introductions. "We call my great-grandfather Great-Daddy. It is rather confusing, Lincoln, because my grandfather is also alive and well and picking peaches in the valley, like Great-Daddy did up to the age of ninety."

"*Tot een en negentig,*" the old man corrected him unexpectedly. The *g* sounds in Afrikaans grated like gravel in his throat.

"Okay, up to the age of ninety-one," Manfred repeated calmly.

"That's amazing," said Lincoln. "At ninety-one my great-granddad back in Atlanta started writing a children's book. It was about a hippopotamus and a crocodile. But he died before he could finish it."

"What a pity that he could not finish it," said Manfred's great-grandfather. "Perhaps you should."

Lincoln stared at the old man. Their eyes met.

Manfred stroked his great-grandfather's arm affectionately. "Have you had something to eat yet, Great-Daddy?"

"Black coffee and a buttermilk rusk," he replied. "Round about ten o'clock. Your ma had left for work. But some dog jumped right over the lower half of the kitchen door and into the house. The upper half was open; it was so hot in here. I gave it some of the rusk."

Manfred grinned at Lincoln. "I told you my great-granddad's English is great!" he said. "But when a reporter from the newspaper came for an interview with him, he sat here with his mouth shut!"

"I didn't feel like speaking English to *that* fellow," the old man said with a tiny, toothless smile.

Manfred shrugged. He disappeared into an adjacent room, reappeared with a clothes hanger, and arranged his shirt on it. "That dog didn't bother Das, did it, Great-Daddy?"

Lincoln's body stiffened. The inconceivable had happened. He had forgotten about Manfred's snake.

"Where is it?" he spluttered.

"Over there," said Manfred's great-grandfather. "Under the firewood."

Manfred beckoned at Lincoln. "Would you like to—"

"No," protested Lincoln. "Let sleeping dogs lie. Let sleeping snakes—"

"—die peacefully." Manfred grinned. "That's what my cousin says. Don't worry. Das is the gentlest reptile this side of the Sahara. Get rid of your things, Lincoln. Chuck them into that room over there. I'm going to fix us something to eat. Will omelet do, Great-Daddy? Would you like some, too, Lincoln?"

"Sure," Lincoln said.

Manfred's head disappeared into the refrigerator. "No *koeksisters* left?" came his voice.

"Nope," replied the old man. "*Alles op.* Your sisters took them."

"*Ag,* no," said Manfred. "Typical. Why is it so dark in here?"

"What are you looking for, Manfred?" asked the old man.

"The green bowl. Ma didn't use all of the egg last night."

127

Ma didn't use all of the egg last night? Lincoln winced. There was only one type of egg on earth that could be poured into a bowl and whisked to be used for last night's supper and today's omelet. Manfred was going to make him eat ostrich egg.

Lincoln walked into the adjoining room. It was sparsely furnished: two beds with gray blankets draped over the mattresses, a pile of gray blankets on the couch in the corner, two old milking stools, a handmade mat, a wardrobe with a cracked mirror on its door. No toys, no pictures against the walls, no curtains. No computer, of course.

Whose bedroom was this? He knew the answer. This was the room he would share with Manfred, his elder brothers, and the twin sisters, Lila, the athlete, and Hannah, the shy one. There would be no personal space, no privacy.

But Manfred was laughing his head off in the kitchen. He was telling his great-grandfather one of his silly jokes. The old man was laughing too. His laughter sounded like a door creaking on its hinges.

Back in D.C., when the father of Lincoln's close friend Julie had been laid off, she was quiet and miserable for weeks. One day, just before Christmas, she blurted out, "Christmas. Big deal. Who cares? There's nothing as awful as getting jeans and cheap sneakers for Christmas. No computer games, no cell phone, just stupid things wrapped up as gifts."

Their friend Richard had tried to cheer her up, probably just making things worse. "You'll survive. Things aren't . . . well, things aren't so important, really."

"Wait until you get sneakers for Christmas and then tell me that," Julie had said glumly.

"I know how you feel," Lincoln had said to her. "My grandmother once gave me six pairs of socks and a comb—a *comb*, of all things!—for Christmas. It did not feel like a Christmas gift at all."

Manfred and his great-grandfather were phenomenal. How could they laugh that way?

Lincoln breathed deeply and walked back into the dark kitchen, where Manfred's great-grandfather was wiping the happy tears from his face. "Let's eat later," he was saying. "Rather do my leg. The ulcer is oozing. Hannah was in a hurry this morning, poor thing."

"The twins always have excuses," Manfred said with a shake of his head. "The same thing happened last time. You should have told Ma or me."

"Your ma gets no rest," replied the old man. "She nearly missed the taxi this morning. If the boy from Washington won't mind—" He cast Lincoln a toothless smile.

For the first time Lincoln noticed the frayed bandage around the old man's leg. He tried not to shake his head at the thought of anybody having to touch such a stained piece of material.

"Lincoln won't mind," said Manfred. "He is from the United States, but he is just an ordinary *oke*."

Lincoln was startled. Just an ordinary *oke*?

"Ouch!" The old man grimaced. Manfred was trying to pull the bandage from his leg.

"Sorry, Great-Daddy. I don't want to hurt you, but this dressing—"

"You should wet it before removing it," Lincoln suggested hoarsely. "My mom is a nurse. When dressings stick to oozing sores, she dissolves a teaspoonful of salt into some lukewarm water and wets the bandage and the gauze underneath it first. It comes off much easier then."

The old man had turned his head. "You should go out of your way to keep this friend, Manfred," he said gently.

"Remember what I told you about this *oke*?" Manfred poured water from the kettle into a jug. He knelt in front of the old man, put his great-grandfather's slippered foot on his skinny knee, and did as Lincoln had said. Little by little he removed the soiled dressing from the old man's sticklike leg.

When the last layer of gauze came off, Lincoln had to suppress a retch at the sight of the putrid sore underneath.

"Now this," said Manfred, "is the limit. The twins—" He got up from his knees. "Come along, Lincoln. We'll be back in a sec, Great-Daddy."

Manfred took a pair of scissors from a hook against the kitchen wall. "If that ulcer is not treated with fresh antiseptic gel and disinfectant—"

A movement, leisurely and slithery like that of a reptile appearing from and disappearing into some unknown swamp, caught Lincoln's eye.

"Das!" exclaimed Manfred. "Bad timing. Great-Daddy does not like the snake to be around when that sore is open like that. Das once wrapped himself round Great-Daddy's leg while I went gel picking. He was in an affectionate mood. Great-Daddy nearly went through the ceiling."

He stooped and caught the *skaapsteker* just below its head. Ever so casually he draped the gleaming body over his shoulder. The snake spiraled energetically, twining itself around Manfred's neck.

Lincoln shuddered.

"Das is hungry," announced Manfred. "Let's get the gel." He opened the lower half of the divided kitchen door and the heat from outside hit them like steam escaping from a pressure cooker.

"Are you going to the drugstore with that snake draped around your neck?" stammered Lincoln. But Manfred stared at him blankly.

"What do you mean?"

"You said we were going to buy some gel."

"I never said that. We are going to pick some gel. Or cut some. Come on, Lincoln. It's not far." Manfred pointed at a thorny plant among the rocks on the slope of the hill behind the house. "That is an aloe plant. The leaf is filled with gel. In that gel and in the juice that drips from it when you cut it, there are lots and lots of healing substances. It's the only thing we use to relieve itching and to heal wounds. My sisters should have got some for Great-Daddy's ulcer ages ago."

He started climbing up to the aloe plant. The *skaapsteker* suddenly uncoiled its body. But Manfred got hold of its throat. "*Ag*, no, Das," he said. "You are making a nuisance of yourself. You can't go lizard hunting now. We haven't got time to sit here waiting for you. Great-Daddy needs us."

Never in his life would Lincoln forget the horror and the heart-stopping simplicity of the next remark:

"Lincoln will just have to hold you while I get the gel."

One second later, Lincoln was holding the wriggling snake by its throat.

He uttered a sound, a panicky muffled cry, but Manfred was snipping away at a young aloe leaf. "He is strong willed," he said over his shoulder. "He does not really like being held by the throat. Let him wind himself around your neck. It feels good, kind of silky."

Yellow drops were dripping from the aloe leaf. Lincoln caught the smell of the gel inside: a pungent, wild odor. The *skaapsteker's* tail swished past his face like a whip.

Having a snake inspecting your shoulders and neck was like having a blackout, coming to, and then experiencing a whole series of blackouts.

"Let's be quick," Manfred was saying. "The gel is best when applied straight from the plant."

"Yes, let's be quick," Lincoln gasped. His whole body was shaking; his legs were wobbly and weak. Everything was blurring. For a fraction of a second—he could almost swear to it—the coiling, twisting *skaapsteker* sported four heads and eight very mean eyes.

"Das hates the smell of aloe gel," Manfred informed him. "He'll calm down, though." He slipped past

Lincoln, yellow aloe juice dripping from the plump leaves. "Take your time, Lincoln. I just want to get to Great-Daddy as fast as possible."

Lincoln was halfway down the path when an uproar from behind startled him. He turned, and beyond the *skaapsteker*'s probing head he saw the faces of five of his classmates: two boys with amazed expressions and three girls. They had popped up from behind a hillock. They must have followed one of the many footpaths crisscrossing the rough and rocky countryside. One of the girls was pointing at the *skaapsteker* coiled around his neck. "Aren't you scared?" she stammered.

Please remember to notify my friends in Washington that I died with a snake's head resting on mine. But the small, awestruck group of classmates had formed a semicircle behind him. There was no butting, no jostling, no shoving, no elbowing.

"Doesn't that thing make your flesh creep?"

"Not really," said Lincoln, breathing slowly and suppressing a mammoth shudder. "It—it feels good. Kind of silky."

He walked calmly into Manfred's house. He could hear them talking softly somewhere on the hillock behind his back, but respectfully.

Manfred had sliced the leaf open. Lincoln was amazed

at the deftness of his friend's fingers, at the gentleness of his touch as he placed the inside of the slit leaf on the open ulcer. "Does it feel good?" Manfred was looking up into the old man's face. Great-Daddy's smile was genuine and beautiful.

"Just what the doctor ordered," the old man said. "The doctor also said that my"—he groped for the right word and found it—"that my great-grandson should be the male nurse."

"Please hold the snake, Manfred." Lincoln made his voice as casual as possible. "My mom showed me how to do a figure eight. I'll demonstrate it to you."

"What is a figure eight?" Manfred asked.

"Just a nice way of wrapping the bandage around someone's leg." Lincoln handed Das to its owner. One brave thing down. Another coming right up. "There's some kind of symmetry to it. My mom says it feels more comfortable to the patient."

"This thing . . . this bandage is dirty," the old man said apologetically.

"That's okay." What was happening? Why did he want to be part of this?

"We should have got a new bandage ages ago," the old man was saying.

"It's okay, Great-Daddy," whispered Lincoln. "For now." He did not know why he was whispering, but it felt right.

Manfred moved toward the wall, making room for Lincoln and stroking the snake.

"It's quite simple, really," said Lincoln. "You hold the bandage like this—" He could feel the fragile bones inside the old man's leg. He looked up and saw the old man smiling at him: a grateful, kindly smile.

"So your father is an . . . "

" . . . exile," Manfred helped him.

" . . . an exile who has come home?" The old man aimed a parrotlike gaze at Lincoln.

Lincoln nodded.

"Are you glad?" the old man asked.

Lincoln could hear his heart thumping in his chest, but not because of the snake performing an Olympic coil round Manfred's neck.

This was it. He could still reject this continent. He could still deny that this was also his homecoming. Or he could hold a *skaapsteker*, touch a sticklike leg, be proud of being called an *oke*, reach out.

For this moment—despite all the known and unknown things he would still have to face—he knew his answer.

"Yes," he said. "Yes, I'm glad we came."

What I Did on My Summer Safari

BY STEPHANIE STUVE-BODEEN

FOR MY SIXTH-GRADE GRADUATION PRESENT I'D expected something useful in a nice box. Instead I got a major inconvenience, batteries not included and postage due. My dad was a diplomat, and we'd spent the last year living in a huge five-bedroom, four-bath house in Dar es Salaam, Tanzania. Our cook and maid lived right with us, which made living pretty easy indeed. We hadn't seen much of the country, so my parents decided to give me a safari for graduation.

Practically all the Americans at the embassy had been to the Serengeti, which meant staying in fancy lodges at night and driving around in air-conditioned vans during the day, getting their fill of lions and leopards and zebras. But we were off to the Ruaha, a little-known and even less traveled national park in the central highlands of Tanzania. My dad insisted it would be a crash course in the culture and landscape of the country we'd called home for almost a year.

We packed up the Toyota Land Cruiser with our tents, sleeping bags, food and drink from the American Embassy commissary, my six-year-old brother, Nate, and my dad's mom, Gramma Larson, who was visiting from Milwaukee.

There's a misconception among the *wazungu*, us foreigners, that safari means driving around, looking at animals. While that's a common use of the word, the literal translation of safari is, simply "a journey." At the start of our safari, which began about o'dark-thirty in the morning, Dad was beside himself. Freed of his three-piece suit and tie, he was dressed in khakis, T-shirt, and hat straight out of Banana Republic.

Mom stayed loyal to the culture and wore a summer dress that covered her thighs, preventing any scandalous glances from passing her way. Despite Mom's admonishing "Sarah!" I'd left my own stash of culturally appropriate dresses at home, preferring shorts and a tank top. I wanted to feel like an American tourist. Nate wore his usual jeans, T-shirt, and Cubs hat, and carried his well-worn copy of *African Wildlife Facts*. Reading it nonstop, he was constantly spouting gems like "A lion's roar can be heard up to five miles away." But he was generally a go-with-the-flow kind of kid. Gramma, never one to go with any flow other than her own geriatric one, was in her typical red polyester pantsuit and white orthopedic shoes, her freshly permed silvery hair protected by a white scarf.

About an hour past Morogoro, I told Dad I needed to use the bathroom. Dad stopped the car along the road, nothing but trees and fields in sight.

"Huh?" I asked.

Mom handed me a roll of toilet paper. "There's a good tree over there."

"I would like a bathroom," I said.

"This is as close as you get," said Dad with what I could have sworn was a very amused expression on his face.

Safari Tip Number One: There are no rest areas in Tanzania.

"Fine." I grabbed the Charmin and walked behind a tree. I had just squatted down and started to do my thing when Nate yelled, "The puff adder only bites when you step on it!"

I heard a rustle in the brush and finished what I was doing rather quickly, then ran back to the vehicle. Nate was laughing his head off, and I punched him. He stuck out his tongue and went back to playing Donkey Kong on his GameBoy. I found my CD player and punched PLAY. I watched through the clear cover as the disc rotated a couple times, then slowed to a stop. "Do we have any batteries?"

"Sarah, they're in the gray container I asked you to load last night," said Mom. When I didn't say anything, she asked, "You did load it, didn't you?"

Safari Tip Number Two: If you are going to be responsible for leaving a box behind, make sure nothing in it belongs to you.

I put my useless CD player back in my bag.

When we reached the town of Iringa, we stopped at an outdoor restaurant called Mama Lulu's. By that time, Gramma Larson had to use a rest room, so I went with her. I waited outside as she opened a creaky aluminum door. I heard her soft "Oh, lordy."

Safari Tip Number Three: While traveling in Tanzania, the outdoor bathrooms are much cleaner than the indoor ones.

Gramma decided she could hold it until we were back on the road and had found a good spot.

The journey to the Ruaha began just out of Iringa. The road was about a sidewalk wide and made strictly of sand. "How far is it?" I asked.

"About sixty miles to the Fox Camp," replied Dad.

Not so bad, I thought. Until I noticed that Dad was going less than thirty miles an hour, and the back of the Toyota was still shimmying like crazy in the loose sand. I looked straight ahead and could see the road forever, going on and on until it became a tiny ribbon that finally met the horizon. We were an hour past Iringa when the Toyota first hesitated. Gramma said, under her breath, "Oh, lordy." We began jerking a tad more regularly, like about every ten seconds. Then, with one final, violent, burping convulsion, our vehicle stopped. Dad got out and looked under the hood.

Safari Tip Number Four: Don't ever have car trouble in the middle of nowhere.

We happened to be parked on a slight incline, so, with Gramma steering, Mom, Dad, and I got behind the Toyota and started pushing. It got moving and we jogged behind it, catching up to push it enough to keep it rolling. After about a quarter mile, we saw a sign in

Swahili. I recognized the words *Wanyama Porini*. "Wild animals," I said. A small track led off to the right. I asked, "Are we sure about this?" but Gramma had already turned the Toyota and we coasted into an encampment. Several Tanzanian men immediately came out of a large tent, brandishing guns. Dad, Mom, and I stopped in our tracks, but the Toyota, with Nate in the back and Gramma steering, continued to roll on its course, stopping just in front of the men. Gramma then completely outdid all lions on the continent by blasting an "OH, LORDY" that could have been heard five point one miles away.

One of the men pointed at Gramma and said something in Swahili. They all laughed and put down their guns. Dad, who had used Swahili more than the rest of us, managed to find out that we were in an anti-poaching camp. Better than a pro-poaching camp, definitely.

We decided to camp for the night. Gramma was going to sleep in the vehicle, and after I heard some strange sounds in the trees that surrounded us, I wanted to join her. The anti-poachers started a fire for us, and Mom threw in some tinfoil-wrapped potatoes and warmed up a canned ham. We gave our hosts several cans of Dr Pepper, which, by the look on their faces, they had never tasted before.

We sat in front of the flames for a long while, listening

to the quiet of the night. On my way to find some more wood to burn, I saw a huge paw print in the dirt.

Safari Tip Number Five: National parks in Tanzania are not at all like zoos.

I crawled into my sleeping bag and looked up at the glow of moon that shone through the thin layer of tent. Nate lined his sleeping bag up next to mine. He said, "Do you know lions have retractable claws? They're much sharper than nonretractable claws."

"Good for them." I shut my eyes.

Nate sighed. "I bet those claws are sharp enough to slice right through the walls of this tent."

I opened my eyes. "Is lion class over now?"

"Oh, don't worry. For about twenty-one hours of the day, lions don't do anything."

I breathed out and shut my eyes. "That's comforting."

Nate continued, "Yeah. It's those three hours before dawn that you have to worry about."

Still utterly not asleep, I smacked him. "Stop!"

"Only one in four hunts are successful, not a very good percentage."

"Finally, some good news," I said.

"Yeah," Nate said. "Although we wouldn't be considered a hunt. We're pretty much a sit-down, all-you-can-eat buffet."

"Mom!" I yelled.

Mom called back from beside the fire, "Go to sleep, Nate."

I really hoped there weren't any lions around—I did not want my first sighting to be just before I was mauled to death. Needless to say, I didn't get much sleep.

In the morning, Mom passed out Pop-Tarts and poured cups of boiled water, but I sneaked a can of root beer.

Safari Tip Number Six: Lukewarm soda beats lukewarm boiled water any day of the week.

The anti-poachers helped us push the Toyota back out to the road, then disappeared into the bush. We started pushing again, as we had the day before, then I heard a car coming. Our Toyota was blocking the road, but we all hollered and waved anyway.

The people were Italian tourists and they tied a rope to our bumper. We hopped into the Toyota, on our way once more. But we went down a dip, got too close to their car, and when they tried to go up the next rise, the rope snapped. The Italians said they'd go ahead and send someone back.

Dad banged his head against the steering wheel a few times. Then he got out of the car and, like a cartoon gone horribly wrong, proceeded to throw his hat on the ground and jump up and down on it. His dignity was not fully functioning. Gramma and Mom didn't even notice, they were so busy wiping the sweat off their faces.

Safari Tip Number Seven: Funny thing, when the car doesn't work, neither does the air conditioning.

The heat was wet, so humid I could feel it dripping down my face, even without my sweat. The sun was too brutal to go outside, so we rolled down the windows and hoped for a breeze. With the windows down we had a new problem: tsetse flies. They had a nasty bite, and they were hearty little suckers. You couldn't just swat them like American flies. You had to smash and twist, preferably with a sturdy object like a shoe. After killing about thirty of them, I realized I hadn't heard from Nate in a while.

When I turned around, Nate was sitting on top of a cooler. He'd obviously given up trying to fight the black swarm because sweat was running down his face and flies were crawling all over him. He looked like a kid on those commercials about feeding third-world countries, only chunkier and better dressed. I clambered over the seat, and we retreated under a mosquito net.

Near midafternoon, a rusty old dump truck came lumbering over the hill, backed around, and stopped in front of us. Three Tanzanians jumped out, and Dad helped them tie a rope to our car. I wanted to say "Tried that!" but I just held Nate and hoped for the best. Of course, the rope broke, so one of the men trimmed it off and tied it back on, but the rope was too short.

Another man got out an ax. He cut down a small tree and tied some of the rope to either end and fastened the tree between the dump truck and our Land Cruiser.

Safari Tip Number Eight: If you don't have a rope, use a tree.

Progress was slow in the sand with all that weight, and I held my breath hoping it would work. Plus the exhaust from the truck was pouring right in our open windows, so not breathing turned out to be the more pleasant option. Slowly, steadily, we finally reached the Ruaha River. Being that the dry season was at hand, the dump truck towed us right through the parched riverbed. Up the other side, I saw smoke. "The men told me there are fires in the park," said Dad.

When we finally arrived at the mechanic's shop, it was almost dusk. Dad arranged to have the Toyota fixed, then be delivered to us at Fox Camp. He told us to grab what we could carry and get in the dump truck. He and one of the men pushed Gramma, whose white scarf was now gray, up into the cab with the driver and Mom.

Nate and I perched in the back of the truck while Dad climbed in and a man handed up our bags. The sun had just set as we started off on our bumpy ride, but the sky was red from the fires. Nate stood on one side of Dad, and I sat on the other. I could smell the smoke as we traveled, and I hoped the whole park wouldn't go up in flames.

"Look!" cried Nate.

I sat up on my knees, so I was just tall enough to look over the edge of the truck. A herd of zebras stood near the side of the road, looking up at us. They began to look gray, their stripes becoming camouflaged in the dimming light. A bit farther were several giraffes. We were nearly eye level in our unconventional safari vehicle, and they simply stood, chewing and gazing, as we went along our noisy way.

Dad said, "Oh, lordy," and we laughed until the tears rolled down our faces. Despite being hot and sweaty and covered with dirt and bug bites from the day's horrific journey, we had just seen our first African animals, in the wild, and we felt glorious.

Safari Tip Number Nine: A safari in a dump truck is still a safari.

The trip to Fox Camp took about an hour, and with the moon coming up through the light haze of smoke, we were able to see more zebra, some hyenas, and we heard an elephant trumpet, although we didn't see any. Through the dark, I saw eyes glittering in the endless expanse beyond us, and could only imagine what creatures they belonged to.

As I slipped into crisp sheets at Fox Camp that night, feeling freshly clean from my only shower in two days, I heard my first lion. There were stone walls between the lion and me, but this was clearly his turf. The roar resonated through my body, like a vibration from nature itself. I shut my eyes and listened, no, *felt* the lion's roar again, answered this time by another. It went on and on, those lions in the night, before I finally fell asleep.

Safari Tip Number Ten: Whoever said it was oh so right—Inconvenience is adventure, wrongly considered.

Her Mother's Monkey

BY AMY BRONWEN ZEMSER

WHATEVER THE SPECIES OF INJURED ANIMAL THAT arrived at the front gate in the arms of a stranger—a pangolin suffering from lethargy, an egret with a defunct wing, a civet that would not eat—Francine's father could never turn it away. To her mother's great consternation, her father would pay the stranger's asking price and carry the scratching or squirming or yowling patient to the back of the yard, where he would tend to its ailments in a convalescence shed beneath the shady leaves of the banana tree. It was in this shed, made from gray brick and cement, that Francine's father would try for many days to relieve the animals of their strange and inexplicable ills, usually without success. Her father was merely an English teacher of the middle grades, hardly a veterinarian, and it was many a terrible evening that Francine and her little sister would observe in sorrow as the pangolin sighed his last breath . . . or the feral cat mewed her saddest good-bye. And almost too frequently to bear, it seemed, Francine and her little sister would return home from school in the afternoon just in time to find that one of the baby guinea pigs had shivered himself away to a more peaceful place . . . or the mongoose had gone stiff with rigor mortis, her frail legs pointing skyward toward the heavens.

"He'll kill off every species in Nimbah County," Francine overheard her mother telling the cook one evening, while her father bid another traveler good-bye and headed toward the backyard with a limp iguana in tow. Her mother's words sounded cold and hard, it was true, but Francine and her little sister quietly believed that she was right, for the only living thing their father had managed to keep alive since their arrival in West Africa was an alarmingly large cockroach that had fallen out of her screaming sister's ear on their third morning in Monrovia. In awe of the roach's tenacity, Francine's father had made it a home out of a large shoebox and placed it on the veranda, where it lived in hero's quarters on the corner of the folding table, a courageous explorer come home to rest after a long passage out the ear canal.

The start of the dry season, with its arid winds and dusty air, had marked the beginning of her family's year in Liberia. The month of September came and went, and October arrived, and still Francine and her little sister remained petless because Francine's father was unable to sustain the life of any creature beyond that of an insect. Then one night a local boy named Morris, who came to the gate whenever he had a pretty hairpin or colored basket to sell, arrived after nine o'clock with a new creature clinging pitifully, and screaming shrilly, into his twisted and worn shirt collar.

The thing was a tiny baby monkey, no larger than a child's hand, with a rust-colored underside that matched the hue of the path beneath Morris's bare feet. Its tail was the color of basalt, save for the very tip, which was bright with blood. The infant had been clutching his mother's breast at the very moment a hunter's bullet penetrated them both, only grazing the tail of the younger, but killing the elder, as they fell from a tall tree and landed on the jungle floor.

Francine's father paid Morris for the monkey, and thanked him, and told him he could go, but the boy was curious and invited himself onto the veranda where the branches of the mango tree grew low and hung over the marble tiles. He stayed while Francine and her little sister gathered around to watch, as did the old night watchman, who had just arrived for his shift. The cook left her boiling fufu in a pot in the kitchen to see what the fuss was about, and even Francine's mother eventually abandoned her garden on the north side of the house, where she had been monitoring her plums, to witness the examination.

"Oh, poor, hideous thing," Francine's mother said in a mixture of horror and empathy as her father peeled the monkey away from his chest and pressed him to the table. The animal cried pitifully beneath the overhead light and struggled to jump up and grab at her father, much in the same way, Francine supposed, that only a few days earlier he had held on to his own dead mother. At first no one, not Francine, or her little sister, or the old night watchman, or Morris, could determine the reason for the monkey's screams. True, a piece of the end of the tail was missing, and the fur around the edges of the wound was matted with filth and blood, but it looked like old blood, and could not have been, Francine's father's said, the cause for such agony. He looked at the monkey from all angles, from the right and left, and lifted the arms, and checked the curled feet and toes, and Francine's mother, impatient and anxious, informed her father that the entire neighborhood would have to be fitted for hearing aids if he did not "shut the little monster up soon."

At last her father isolated the source of the monkey's anguish, and everyone drew near, and looked, and they were deeply horrified at what they saw. The last finger, the tiniest finger on the right hand, which was no larger than a matchstick, swayed precariously by a slender thread of skin, like a broken twig holding on at the bark. Francine shuddered mightily. Her little sister wept. And into the diminishing heat of the evening, long after Francine's little sister was dragged whining to bed, and her mother had stopped insisting that the infant monkey, like all the other animals in her father's care, would never wake to see the sun creep over the edges of the mango leaf, Francine's father leaned over the table and tended to his unquiet sufferer. Hours passed, and the cook packed up her fufu and rice into Tupperware containers and left, and Morris grew bored, and went home. Only Francine remained with her father, watching in silence as the night bore heavily upon them, layering the veranda in darkness.

Her father found a stick in the front of the yard and, using a sharp knife, whittled the wood down to the width of a flat toothpick. He applied an antiseptic from a bottle Francine retrieved from the medicine cabinet in the bathroom. Next, using thread from around a spool, he pressed the wayward finger to the front of the wood, fashioning a miniature splint. The monkey screamed in outrage. When Francine's father finished, he held the exhausted creature close to his breast, and spoke softly to him, and assured him of his strength and resilience. After all, her father said, the monkey was still a baby, and had the benefit of youth to assist him in the healing process.

The night had gone more deeply into darkness. "Time for bed," Francine's father said.

"But will he live?" Francine asked, remembering suddenly the poor mongoose, supine and withered with death, at the bottom of the cage in the convalescence shed.

"We'll see," her father replied, wearily. He was sitting in a chair on the veranda, his chin dropping to his chest from exhaustion. The infant stirred in his arms and slept. Francine obeyed, somewhat anxiously, and went to bed.

In the gray of the next morning, before the thinnest

light revealed itself to a lonely papaya growing in the yard, her father woke them. He whispered that both she and her sister should tiptoe down the hall and out of the house to the backyard and the convalescence shed. Francine and her sister came and saw, and were amazed, and so delighted, because unlike the lethargic pangolin, or the egret with the defunct wing, or the civet that would not eat, the baby monkey had in fact lived. No longer crying, or even whimpering, he held out his arms to them from in between the wooden slats of his cage and looked at them with bright, wide-open eyes. Francine experienced a surge of real happiness, and her little sister clapped her hands and hopped all around the yard.

"He should stay in his cage at night," Francine's father said, "for safety. But during the day he can roam the yard. The fence is high enough. And he's too young to think of wandering off." Her father explained that the baby monkey would need a healthy diet and proper exercise, and that he was to remain in the cook's charge while Francine and her little sister were at school. In the afternoons the monkey was the girls' responsibility. The cook was not at all pleased at the idea of baby-sitting a juvenile primate, and voiced her opposition plainly, but Francine's father wouldn't hear any more of it and went into the house to sleep. Francine and her little sister took turns holding the monkey, every so often stopping to argue over who got to hug the adorable thing next, or to kiss his little face, until their mother came out of the house and reminded them that their education would not be held in recess while the two of them squabbled over who was next to have a turn at feeding a morsel of squashed banana to a hairy baby.

So it was that a baby monkey took up residence at Francine's house. The dry season persisted throughout the winter months, and the earth was parched, and longed for rain. The baby monkey grew, and shiny fur covered the end of his tail, and the finger adhered to the hand. Soon there were no visible reminders of his hardship in the jungle. He was a happy monkey, quick and adroit, with remarkably humanlike features that amazed Francine and her little sister. He could peel a banana in seconds flat, or undo the clasp on Francine's lunch box before she even discovered the box was missing. Once, the mischievous animal even pushed back the bolt that locked his cage at night, inspiring Francine's father to build another cage—a larger, better one, with room for a swing and some branches—beneath the shady leaves of the banana tree. Francine's father was very proud of the youthful primate and named him Angus, which meant He Who Has Unique Strength, and considered him, with the exception of the humble cockroach, his greatest achievement. The only real curiosity, it seemed, Francine thought as she walked along the muddy path cutting through a village of homes thatched together with mud and straw, was that Angus merely tolerated Francine and her little sister. He didn't even love Francine's father, to whom Francine believed he owed his life. No, oddly enough, it was Francine's *mother* that Angus loved most dearly, most passionately and inexplicably, above anyone else in the household.

"Girls, girls, I beg you," their mother would cry, attempting to lift Angus from her head the way an old queen might try to remove a heavy crown at the end of a long day's reign. "Please remove this nimble beast. It's snarling my hair." And Francine and her little sister would try in vain to pull the monkey away from her mother, but he would chatter and scream so piercingly, so menacingly, that Francine often wondered if the act served as a terrible reminder of the day he was so ruthlessly separated from his real mother.

"Never mind," her mother would finally say, allowing Angus to travel down her arm and into her straw bag, where there was sure to be a cellophane-wrapped candy waiting for him. He would swiftly untwist the wrapping and stuff it into his cheek, where it would stay, a hard knot on one side of his face that bulged and stuck out, giving him a comical appearance.

Angus followed their mother wherever she went and was utterly impervious to her insults. "Oh, go away, you filthy monster," she was overheard uttering while hoeing the cassava during the month of January, as Angus perched on her shoulder, preening her hair. Or, "Nasty, ugly thing," she would say while picking guavas in February, pausing only two or three times to hand an overripe fruit to her furry companion.

Francine's mother detested the "hirsute beast" while cutting stalks of sugarcane in March. She abhorred him in April as she clipped the okra, giving him the leaves to chew, and loathed him more in May while peeling mangos for the jam. Francine and her little sister hid behind the crinum lillies and watched her drop the yellow-orange mango skins into Angus's open palms. In June she hated him and fed him soursop, and in July, one of the rainiest months, when it was too wet to be outside to hoe or cut or clip, she called him a "greedy thing," and hugged and kissed him, and fed him sandwiches of bread and honey.

So went the remainder of the rainy season, with its moist evenings following drenched afternoons, and drenched afternoons following dewy mornings. Then it was August, time for the soggy sun to show her face again, and for Francine's father to remind them that their year in Liberia was coming to an end. Soon they would need to find suitable new employment for the cook and a new home for the old night watchman to guard.

"Of course Angus will need a new home, too," her father said.

"Well, of course," Francine's mother echoed, with some nastiness. "Did you think I was planning on taking the hairy nuisance with me?" But later that evening Francine saw her mother sitting in the old wooden chair on the veranda, smoothing Angus's fur, which shone now, and staring quietly into a tiny moon.

Two weeks passed, and Francine and her little sister began to remove their books from the shelves and their toys and games from the closets. Rugs and lamps were given away, and a framed pen-and-ink sketch was taken from its place above the sofa, and sold. The carpet in the front room was rolled up and put aside, revealing the cold marble tiles beneath. Suitable employment was arranged for the cook.

Again the sun rose, and fell again, and shed its light upon the papaya tree beneath Francine's window. One Saturday morning, after Francine's father had gone to school to pack his papers into boxes, and while Francine's little sister was playing with Morris in the yard, her mother went and found Angus, where he was annoying the cook as she hung the laundry, and took him, and told Francine to get into the car.

They were going to see the Swedish man, was all Francine's mother would say as she gripped the steering wheel of the Mazda on their way down Old Road in the direction of Chugbor. Francine held Angus in her lap, who struggled and reached for her mother. Her mother did not speak. Instead she looked straight ahead at the road in front of the car while Francine sat, tense and afraid, and waited for what would come next. A short while later, Francine's mother turned onto a long, unpaved road shaded on either side by tall palms. The road ended in a square tract of dusty, yellow parking lot. There were a few old cars parked to one side, and some Liberian children chasing a rusty tire with sticks in front of a tall gate made out of metal. The gate was much taller and heavier than the one in front of her own house and it looked as if it were designed to keep people from either coming in or out.

It turned out, to Francine's surprise, that the place was the local zoo, and the Swedish man was the zookeeper. He was tall and lean, with blue eyes, and hair that had gone yellow from years of smoking. It was a small zoo, with a mud path that led visitors around a U-shaped perimeter, starting at the entrance in front of the chimpanzee cages. Dense hibiscus hedges lined the path leading in one direction to the lion cages, then farther on to where the leopards snored. In the other direction Francine could see smaller cages holding different species of snake—green mamba and puff adder and viper—and after that, a sanctuary filled with rice birds. It wasn't an unhappy place. A peacock marched by, exhibiting his feathers, and a baby hippopotamus, no taller than a Labrador, ambled past.

"So this is the Diana monkey," said the Swedish man, confusing Francine for a moment because she had never thought of her pet as anything but Angus. Francine's mother told her to stand by a partition of stones that separated her from the bush rats while she went to confer with the Swedish man in his office, which really was not an office but a large palaver hut. Francine watched the bush rats burrowing into their holes, but they weren't very lively, and she soon grew bored and wandered over in the direction of the palaver hut where she thought she heard a commotion. To her horror, the commotion turned out to be her mother, who was shrieking, "Get away from me, you hideous thing" while frantically attempting to hurl Angus at the Swedish man. Angus screamed and tried to grab at Francine's mother, who hurried away, pulling Francine by the elbow toward the tall gate that pushed out to the bright yellow square of parking lot. The Liberian children were still chasing tire rims with sticks. Francine's mother squeezed her arm tightly and shouted over her shoulder with haughty pride, her brown eyes wide with fury, "The miserable thing likes peanut butter!"

Back in the car, Francine argued with her mother, tears streaming down her face. Why hadn't she told her that Angus was going to the zoo to stay, she wanted to know. Instead of replying, her mother drove on, half muttering, half chanting, " . . . got into the pantry, ate the ripening guavas, tore off the leaves of the almond tree, dug up the garden, climbed over the wall and annoyed the Parisian next door," as if reminding herself of all those grievances, Francine thought, could justify the awful thing she had done.

At dinner that evening, no one, not even Francine's little

sister, dared to speak about Angus, although the yard seemed forlorn and empty without him. Even the cook seemed robbed of purpose without the little pest to swat away from her rice bowl. The family busied itself over the last few days boarding up the remainder of their things. The last few books and toys were packed into cardboard barrels with silver-colored rims to hold the goods in place, and the dishware was wrapped in newspapers, and stacked, and the cutlery was sorted. The day before they were scheduled to leave, Francine's father decided to go back to the zoo, "to check on Angus, to say good-bye."

"Oh, why bother," cried their mother from the pantry in the kitchen, dropping a dish on the tiles, where it shattered. Then, thrusting a peanut-butter-and-honey sandwich into Francine's hand as she followed her father to the car, she added, "He won't remember you. You'll see."

The Swedish man was tending to an ostrich when Francine and her father arrived, but he pointed amiably to the monkey cage, and Francine drew in her breath when she saw all the different monkeys mixed in together, mona monkey and colobus, sooty mangabey and bush baby, all fighting and scrambling and screeching at one another in the large cage. At first Francine did not recognize him, he was so dirty, his fur all matted with excrement and his eyes dulled, but then he turned, and screamed, and rushed forward and flung himself at the bars of the cage, and she knew he remembered. Angus cried and wrung his hands, and ran back and forth on the branch closest to the front of the cage, and held out his arms and tried to reach them. Francine cried, and then wept and pleaded with her father never to leave the continent of Africa so that they could take Angus back home with them to his yard and his banana tree. And Francine's father cried, too, and said that it was impossible. He unwrapped the peanut-butter-and-honey sandwich and held it out to Angus, who took it, hungrily, but a larger monkey knocked him away, and stole it, and ate it.

When they drove away, this time forever, Francine's despair turned into a boiling fury toward her mother, and she demanded an explanation. "But why?" she asked her father, over and over. "Why didn't she come to say good-bye?"

"She couldn't," her father said. "She couldn't have come with us to say good-bye for all the diamonds in the Ivory Coast. Angus stole your mother's heart from the beginning. He was your mother's monkey."

The next day, they closed and locked the front door leading out to the veranda for the last time. A gardener was already trimming the hibiscus hedge so that it would look nice for the new people moving in. The hired driver started the engine to the van that was to take them to the airport, and her father loaded the last suitcase in the back.

"Say good-bye," her father said, getting in the front seat, between the driver and Francine's mother. Francine's little sister began to cry, not because she was sad, but because she had to leave her clamshell puzzle behind; there was no place left to pack it and her mother had said she was too old to keep it anymore. Francine's mother looked out the window of the passenger seat as the driver backed down the driveway, brushing past the branches of the almond tree on his way out the gate. Francine sat behind the driver, next to her little sister, and try as she did, she couldn't tell if her mother was looking at the garden in the back, or the bare clothesline, or if she was looking one last time at Angus's empty cage, the door hanging ajar, beneath the swaying leaves of the banana tree.

an african american

BY MERI NANA-AMA DANQUAH

i wanna tell you a story
of washington, dc
of atlanta, georgia
of addis abbaba
of tangier, soweto and lagos

i wanna shed some light
on the dark continent
i wanna tell you a story
of me

i stand before you
dark and proud
asante princess
african queen
born and bred
on black soil
in a black nation
they call ghana

i spoke the language
of my ancestors
i ate the food
planted by our mothers' hand
i danced the drumbeats
of our animist gods

an asante princess
an african queen
who crossed the middle passage
arrived in america
speaking very little english
with thick lips
and thick accent

unable to pronounce my name
people called me
the foreigner
the african girl
i went to school
with your daughters and sons

your cousins and friends
mimicked their speech
dressed their style
seemingly became one of them

i wove my blackness
my africanness
chameleon-like
into the red, the white and the blue
which is the fabric of this nation
wanting desperately to belong

when i sleep
i snore with the lions and tigers
in the safari land
i snore with the sounds
of the noontime traffic on georgia avenue
in the district of columbia
when i dream
the voices of jomo kenyatta, patrice lumumba
and dr. martin luther king, jr.

speak to me in unison
when i cry
rain falls on the sahara
and the potomac river overflows
i sway to alpha blondy
as easily as i do stevie wonder

open your ears
my children
and listen to this griot
talk of history
being made
i wanna tell you this story
of my life

the blood which flows
through the left side of my body
is the mississippi river
every day i wake it croons
"lift every voice and sing"
the anthem of the american negro

the blood which flows
through the right side of my body
is the nile river
every day i rise it screams out loud
"africa, oh africa, cry freedom
for all your children"

don't think me confused
because i don't know
where home is anymore
i just know
that the veins
in the body from the right and the left
flow to the heart
and become one love

if i die on african soil
bury me in jeans and sneakers
let my tombstone read in english
"native washingtonian"
and sing an old negro spiritual for me please

if i die on american soil
pour libation on the ground
lay a flag of red, green and gold
with a black star
on my coffin
let the talking drums spread the news
let the words on my tombstone
be multi-lingual and let them scream
asante princess
african queen

let no one question my origin
let me live and die in peace
as who i am
because you see
I have broken all barriers
of love and unity
i am
in the truest sense of the word
an african american

My Brother's Heart

BY MAWI ASGEDOM

THE DESERT, I REMEMBER. THE SHRIEKING HYENAS, I remember. Beyond that, I cannot separate what I remember of Ethiopia from what I have heard in stories.

I may or may not remember seeing my mother look at our house in Adi Wahla, Ethiopia, just before we left. Gazing at it as though it were a person she loved. Staggering toward the house's white outside wall, laying her hands on it for a few moments, feeling its heartbeat—feeling her own heartbeat—then kissing it, knowing that she might never see it again.

I remember playing soccer with rocks, and a strange man

telling me and my brother Tewolde that we had to go on a trip, and Tewolde refusing to go. The man took out a piece of gum, and Tewolde happily traded his homeland. I followed, of course. I went wherever my big brother went.

My family—my mother, my older brother, and my younger sister—walked across the desert, surviving hyenas, rebel groups, and disease in search of my father, who was already in the neighboring country of Sudan.

After a few months we found him, and us kids were running around in a Sudanese refugee camp called Umsagata. Umsagata had no paved roads, so it didn't attract many cars. Seven and five years old, Tewolde and I walked or ran everywhere we went.

One time, though, a giant tractor pulled up. It was unlike anything that we had ever seen. Its wheels were the size of small adobes.

After a while, the owner got out and entered a home. We ran over to inspect the tires, wondering if what we had heard was true: that if you took a sharp stone and applied pressure to the tire's little nozzle, you could empty out all the air.

We grabbed little stones and pushed eagerly. Sure enough, the air shot out of the tire like lava from a volcano.

And the owner shot out of the house, shaking his fists in fury. We bolted. For we knew that no tire pumps could be found anywhere nearby. And who wants to be stuck in the middle of Sudan with a flat, giant tractor?

I was still tagging after Tewolde six years later. By now my family lived in Illinois, practically in Michael Jordan's backyard. And almost every day my brother and I made our way to Triangle Park, just over the railroad tracks from where we lived, to watch and play hoops. Each time, we crossed the tracks illegally. We'd heard that there was a fifty-dollar fine if you got caught, but we didn't care. We refused to walk all the way around, more than four hundred yards extra, just to use the crosswalk.

One day we crossed the tracks, walked through the trees, and came out on the other side, across the street from the rectangle that was misnamed Triangle Park. Almost forty Vietnamese and Cambodian refugees, Wheaton College students, and Route 38 brothers milled about the court.

We knew that we would have to wait at least an hour to get a game. We stood on one side of the street, adding our figures to the long line of parking meters that guarded the tracks behind us.

Tewolde. Myself. A giant, light-skinned, Nigerian-

American brother named Big Bo. And a dark-skinned brother with an impressive 'fro, even bigger than the ones that Americans had sported in the '70s. This was the kind of 'fro that Eritrean and Ethiopian *tegadalies*, or guerilla fighters, grew out in the wilderness.

Guerilla-afro brother leaned against the parking meter, and it moved. Not much, but just enough.

Glancing at the sand-speckled dirt next to the meter, and then at one another, each of us considered the same question: How many quarters did that double-headed parking meter hold?

"I bet it holds at least five dollars! Maybe even ten!"

"I bet it holds even more. The meter man probably comes to collect the money every two weeks, and with its two heads, the meter probably collects at least two dollars a day. That's gotta be at least thirty dollars in there."

Thirty divided by four equals seven dollars and fifty cents. Tewolde and I grinned—this could double our annual budget.

From then on, each time we went to Triangle Park, we shook our giant piggy bank just a little more. Each time, we heard our money jingle a little more freely. One day Big Bo became impatient and bull-rushed the meter, knocking it flat on its back.

Pedestrians and cars passed by, commuters coming home after a long day's work in the city. If they saw four brothers standing next to the fallen meter, they would suspect something. If they saw four brothers carrying it, they would call the police. But we refused to leave our parking meter. We had worked too hard for it. And we wanted our seven-fifty.

We picked it up. One parking meter, four teenage guys—no problem, we figured. But the city had weighed down the bottom of the meter with a hundred pounds of cement, making it almost impossible to balance.

We didn't care. It could have been three hundred pounds. Nothing was going to keep us from our money. We dragged our prize to the secret tunnel next to the railroad tracks. Tewolde and I had discovered the tunnel long ago, when we had gone hunting with a Cambodian brother. Slinging homemade bows and arrows, we had patrolled the trees that border the tracks, looking for rabbits and squirrels. Once, we had hit a rabbit and it had led us to the tunnel.

The tunnel was a great underground hideaway. Usually, though, we avoided it because overgrown plants guarded the entrance and darkness reigned inside. Besides, the tunnel was only three feet high.

We crept in slowly, waiting for our eyes to adjust to the dark. We kept dragging the meter until we were sure that no one could see it from the outside. Then we encountered another major problem: We had no way to get the money out. The meter's money pouch had no screws near it. I guess the city had prepared for punks like us.

The next morning, we returned with hammers, screwdrivers, and nails, vowing to find a way into the money pouch. We saw metal tent pegs lying next to the tracks; they would help us to pop open the meter head.

Our hour elapsed, and still we labored. To keep our spirits up, we shook the meter head and listened to the clang of our quarters. Laughing, we considered ourselves the boldest of adventurers. Who could stop us? We were modern-day Robin Hoods, taking from the rich and giving to the poor—which in this case was ourselves.

At some point, I heard a noise. But I thought it was one of the other kids. As the static of a walkie-talkie grew louder, though, I knew. I knew even before I saw the flashlight and the metal star and the policeman's unbelieving white face gazing in at us. I saw felony at age eleven flash before my eyes, and I saw my fear mirrored in my brother's eyes, too.

Even worse, we both thought of my father.

"*My children,*" he would say. "*There was a poor widow who lived in the countryside. She had neither livestock nor garden and lived each day without knowing what or how she would eat the next day. She had only one thing in the world, her young son.*

"*One day the widow's son, who had grown old enough to play outside with his friends, brought home an egg. A tiny egg—small like the dust. The widow did not ask where the tiny egg came from. She boiled it and they ate it together.*

"*The next day the son brought a bigger egg. Soon after, two eggs, then ten eggs. Finally he brought the whole chicken. The widow still said nothing. She kept cooking the food and feeding herself and her son.*

"*Many chickens, sheep, and goats later, the son finally hit the jackpot. He brought home a whole cow. The mother said nothing, and they milked the cow and drank the milk together.*

"*As they sat finishing the milk, the magistrate came with the police and arrested the son for stealing the cow. Declaring that the son would have to die for his crime, the magistrate ordered the police to take him to the house of imprisonment.*

"*Throwing herself at the magistrate's feet, the distraught widow begged for her son's freedom. 'Please, sir, I beg you, he is my only son and all that I have. Please show mercy on him.'*

"*But before the magistrate could speak, the son replied to his mother. 'No, Mother, if you had really cared about me, you should have stopped me when it was only a tiny egg. Now it's too late.'*

"*It starts small, with a tiny egg. But before you know it, the egg becomes a chicken and the chicken, a cow. Then you find yourself in the house of imprisonment or worse.*"

My father would finish, "*So I am telling you now—don't say that your father did not warn you. If I ever catch you stealing the smallest thing, if I hear that you have ever been thinking about stealing anything, fear for your lives. I will make you lost.*"

Having attended church fifty Sundays out of the year and studied the Bible as a family each Saturday and Sunday night, having grown up with our culture's morals implanted in our consciences and, of course, having heard our father's it-starts-with-an-egg fable, we should have feared to steal anything, let alone government property.

But we had not learned our lesson, and we found ourselves staring at a policeman. Had he seen us looking for the tent pegs out on the tracks? Had he discovered the missing parking meter and decided to snoop around? Had a passerby heard that clanging and told him about the noise?

We didn't know. We just knew that it was time to run.

My brother and I had been chased by a dog one summer, chased for two blocks. We had run then.

We had exploded fireworks near a bully's foot one Fourth of July, and he had chased us for half a mile. We had run then.

But never in our lives had we run like we ran from that cop. Keeping our heads low, hoping the policeman wouldn't fit in the tunnel, praying that another policeman did not wait on the other side, the four of us blazed out the far end as if a time bomb ticked behind us.

Tewolde and I sprinted all the way home, flew into our rooms and changed our clothes. Put on a hat! Pat down your hair! Try to look different! Hide in the basement!

And pray that they don't come.

When we were just starting our lives in America, our father told us about strangers. We should always treat them kindly, he said, because they could have been sent by God. He told us stories of how back home in Adi, God's angels would descend out of the mountains and mingle among the people.

But people always mistreated the angels, my father said, because the angels never looked like angels. They were always disguised as beggars, homeless people, and misfits. No matter how abnormal or smelly the strangers, my father always said that they could be angels, given to us by God to test the deepest sentiment of our hearts.

After we arrived in the U.S., my father welcomed an angel who was particularly well disguised. The angel gave off the most ungodly odor, half from his nasty clothes and half from his smudged and muddy body. He walked with a great weariness, as if he were about to collapse with each step, and his spirit had almost abandoned his eyes.

Maybe because my father had been an angel himself so often; maybe because he had survived only by the kindness of those who could see through his disguise; maybe because he had felt the deep pain of homelessness, my father welcomed the man into our home. We fed him and clothed him and gave him shelter.

The angel did not have much. In fact, it looked like he had absolutely nothing. But as he left, he pulled a rainbow-colored address book out of his dirty shirt and handed it to us. We refused, but he insisted. And we accepted. For we knew that the exchange of gifts blesses the giver even more than the receiver. Though we were not familiar with address books and had not used them before, we used his address book to store the addresses and phone numbers of our loved ones for the next several years. And we always thought of him: our angel.

It wasn't until we were teenagers that my brother and I started to understand what angels truly meant. As usual, it was Tewolde who led the way. He left behind the days of stealing parking meters and started to undergo a process my people call *libee migbar*, or developing a heart.

One cold day Tewolde and I made sandwiches—thick, poor-man's ham from Aldi's supermarket, slapped onto wheat bread and slathered with a thin film of mayonnaise—and headed to the public library. As we approached the library's entrance, we saw a dark-haired white brother shivering under the awning where kids usually waited for their parents.

But he was no kid, and no one was coming for him. That's why he was sitting outside in the dead of winter.

We watched his reddish cheeks quiver; we couldn't tell if it was from the cold or from something else. We went to him and asked if he was hungry, and he said, "I lost my job and never got another one, and I don't think I'll ever get another one again. I'm done."

We stared at him, wondering if he was the address-book brother from long ago, but knowing in our hearts that it did not matter. Maybe every stranger was an address-book brother, sent to test the goodness inside us.

Whatever the answer, Tewolde's heart spoke. We should give him our sandwiches. I nodded my head and took the sandwiches out of my backpack. I offered them to him. "I hope you like Aldi ham, bro."

I went inside then, but Tewolde stayed outside and braved the cold with our friend. Eventually Tewolde and I left. I forgot about the man for a year, and I thought my brother had too. I didn't know the truth until the day I found myself following Tewolde again, this time carrying some workout equipment someone had given him. "I have a friend who needs these weights," he told me.

Hoping it wasn't far, I followed. We went across the street—to a nightmarish apartment building I had visited in elementary school. I'd had a friend who lived in the building's cellar; it was the kind of cellar that made me think of turn-of-the-century sweatshops. No lighting. No air. No life. How could such a place exist in America?

We dragged the bench, the bar, and the weights upstairs and knocked on a door. A malnourished man answered, and I tried to remember where I had seen him. But I couldn't place his face.

When he saw my brother, his gaunt, joyless face burst wide with laughter.

"How did you get these?" he asked us, and my brother said we had an extra one. We stayed and talked for a few minutes, and he told us that he was trying to make it, trying to keep his job. But it was hard to have confidence and hope.

As he talked I came to realize who he was. On our way out, I asked my brother, "How did you know where to find the address-book brother from the library? Did you run into him again?"

Before Tewolde answered, I knew the truth.

Tewolde had found him housing and a job, encouraged him, and even given him money—even though my bro had so little himself. Looking at my big brother, I saw that he was once again walking ahead of me into a new place, perhaps even a place where I could never follow. As with the widow's son who had moved from an egg to a chicken to a sheep to a goat to a cow, my brother had experienced his own special transformation, one that would change both our hearts forever.

Flimflam

BY JANE KURTZ

IT SHOULDN'T HURT TO WALK. NOT JUST TO *WALK*. NOT
for an—okay—not glammy, not Ms. Sizzle but (as Mom
would say) perfectly healthy kid like me.

But it does.

Every day, I walk across the commons on my way to
English class. Every day, the wowsers are sitting there
slurping their morning cup of coffee together. Coffee!
Even though they're in ninth grade. And they stare.

Every day, I feel prickles burning the backs of my legs
as I walk. I hunch my shoulders a little, even though I
don't want to. It's almost like I think one of them might

throw a cup of coffee, hitting me smack in the back. I take tiny, wormy steps.

The wowsers never walk this way. They flimflam across the commons with a cool smoothness as if they owned it and charged the rest of us rent. They have no idea how embarrassment feels in perfect broad daylight.

But all of that is about to change. My best friend, Loly, and I have a plan. Loly's real name is Mitselale, but she tells everyone to call her Loly. "Mitselale," she says. "What kind of name is that?"

"What kind of name *is* it?" I asked her once.

"Eritrean."

"What does it mean?"

Loly shrugged. "I have no clue. Ask my grandmother."

Loly lives with her grandmother. She has milky brown skin and huge brown eyes, the kind artistic people draw when they are doodling puppies and other small animals and they want to make you say, "Ooooooo. For CUTE." She's easily the most gorgeous girl in school, but people don't see that because she usually has her head down. Our big plan will change all of that.

"You," one of the wowsers calls suddenly.

I look up so fast I just about give myself whiplash. Instantly I want to crawl into a wormhole. Or maybe just hit myself on the head and put myself out of my misery. No wowser would act like such a boohick anytime *this* decade.

"*You,*" the girl says again. It's Ashleigh Conners. "Are you going to the Screamer concert Saturday night?"

Two of her friends laugh catty ha-has. They are toying with me like I am a mouse, and for an awful second I stand there all doo-dah. But this time I'm ready to toy back. "Right," I say calmly.

Ashleigh stares at me. "Like fun."

"Like true," I say. And it is true. This is the big plan for Loly and me. We had to beg and whine and scrabble all over the ground with my parents and her grand-mother for a month but finally, finally when we prom-ised promised *promised* that we would stick to each other like wallpaper sticks to paste, they agreed. I'm pretty sure Loly's grandma must have hated the idea, because her grandmother is even more boohicky than my parents, but Loly just shrugs when I ask her how she did it.

"I don't believe it," Ashleigh says.

Matt Evans takes a step toward me. "I do," he says. His eyes are sweet green. He is tan even in the middle of winter. He reaches out his arm. His fingers are strong, so strong they look like he bench-presses fifty pounds with them. They curl around my skinny white wrist. I stare down at his tan fingers as if my eyes are about to popcorn out of their eye sockets. "Believe it," he says. He grins at me, a stomach-whirling, wide smile. "I can tell she's no baby." His fingers slip away from my wrist. "See you there, okay?" he says.

I flimflam up the stairs as if my shoes have suddenly been pumped full of hot dancing air. Loly is right there at the top. "You will never this millennium guess what happened," I squeak. My breath pants out of me like I have been running for the presidential fitness award.

"Tell me after your English class, okay? I've got to get ready for algebra." For some reason, Loly is not toasty warm, not like usual. Her voice almost sounds as if she has been crying or will cry sometime soon. Or maybe she's mad.

"Wait," I say, but when she turns around her eyes are so tensified that all I say is, "What did you do in English?"

"The Diary of Anne Frank." Loly curls some of her already-curly hair around one finger and twists and twists it like little kids do. "She was a real girl, you know. Ms. Schill was telling us about the concentration camps."

I tap the friendship bracelet she gave me against the one on her arm that I gave her. "Flee-flee to algebra, then," I say. I smile at her. She doesn't smile back.

I stare after her thinking that I understand. It's so downish to read about something like that. No wonder Loly isn't in the smoothest of moods. I don't get it about Anne Frank. Why would people be so weird and mean to other people? How could anyone take someone who was a kid, like us, and make her into some big *enemy*? Why would normal people just stand around all doo-dah while it happened? Even the wowsers would never do something like that.

But not even this depressing story can ruin my morning. I squeeze into my seat and take the handout the guy in front of me hands back. "In 1933," I read, "the new Chancellor of Germany, Adolf Hitler, looks for ways to stir up resentment, fear, and prejudice against Jewish families. Jews are forbidden to own land. The Nazis post signs saying, 'German people, defend yourselves! Do not buy from Jews,' and boycotts of Jewish businesses begin. In 1938, resentment and prejudice erupt in rage. *Kristallnacht* (Night of the Broken Glass) ends with more than ninety people killed and thousands of homes and businesses destroyed. Mr. Frank is one of the few Dutch Jews to believe that such horrors can reach his family, too."

I sigh. There are a zillion things I would rather think about, and I think about some of them until Ms. Schill's voice bashes through. "Anne, her mother, and her sister are taken to Auschwitz, where Anne's mother dies," she is saying. "My father was one of the U.S. soldiers who liberated that concentration camp. How do you think the soldiers felt as they looked around at walking skeletons, some of them so weak they couldn't even eat the food the soldiers had brought?"

There is flat silence. "Bad?" says Justin in the front row.

"People, people," Ms. Schill says. "Let's develop a little vocabulary. Try fury, frustration, guilt, and despair. The soldiers who saw the camps vowed such a thing would never happen again."

Most kids in the class give little squirms. I, though, go back to floating in my own dream, where Matt Evans is hoo-hahing me around the commons and we are laughing . . . laughing.

"I have the most glammy thing to tell you," I say to Loly the minute I see her after school. "And we have *big* plans to make for the concert. I can't wait a single day longer." I look up and the sunshine has never been this toasty, the trees have never been all shimmer-glimmery this way. It is simply the most gorgeous day there has ever been in any millennium.

I'm still staring at the trees as we start down my sidewalk when Loly turns and looks at me. "Um . . . I need to tell you something," she says shyly. "I—I don't think I'm going."

"To the concert?" I am stunned, shaken, whomped in the gut. But right away I know she'll change her mind once we talk. She's my best friend. Besides, if Ms. Schill has taught me anything this whole year it's about setting and stuff. Bad things never happen to good guys in a story on a sunshine day—when disaster strikes it's always raining or at least cloudy.

"My aunt came from Eritrea last week," Loly says. "Every night she talks to me about . . . things. Did you know that Ethiopia and Eritrea fought for about *thirty years*? Ethiopian planes would bomb in the daytime, so people started living in caves and underground houses and only coming out at night. My aunt says a whole generation of Eritreans became people of the night."

"Fierce!" I say. "Kinda like Anne Frank in the annex, huh? Only the Eritreans had more room." Even though I am itching dying ooooozing with impatience to tell her about Matt and all, I am no clam. I know very well that I have to listen to her and give her all kinds of back pats and she will feel much better. We are warmest-heart friends.

Loly reaches into her backpack and pulls out a newspaper article. She hands it over without looking at me. "They're back at it," she says. I try to read as we walk and then finally sit on my bottom step to finish.

> The women of Eritrea—a tiny country, only as big as Pennsylvania—are hurting again. "Where are my children? Where are my children?" wails one mother as she walks through Barentu. "I fled when the shelling began," she tells an AFP correspondent visiting the town. While running she became separated from her children, aged ten and fourteen.

> In a nearby town, women and children are living under a concrete bridge, in case of shelling. "Where else can we go?" says a woman in her sixties, scrunched under the bridge, waving away swarms of flies with a eucalyptus branch. Women make up a third of the country's armed forces,

fighting in mixed regiments, driving tanks, and flying helicopters. They are excused from front-line action only if they are pregnant.

In 1991, when the tyrant Haile Mariam Mengistu fell as president of Ethiopia and fled to Zimbabwe, the women of Eritrea stood in their villages howling with delight. At that point, everyone believed peace with Ethiopia was here to stay. After all, Zenawi Meles, the new Ethiopian prime minister, has an Eritrean mother. When Eritrea held its vote for independence from Ethiopia, women in bright scarves threw showers of popcorn over international observers and chanted and clapped with joy.

Those women will again take to the battlefields, the caves, the mountains, and wait, even if it takes another thirty years. They will not be defeated, but the Horn of Africa will once more become a burial ground for the women and their families. Someone must speak for peace, for the children, and for the hungry of both Ethiopia and Eritrea. So far, the United States is doing practically nothing. One senior official confidentially says that this is considered a "nuisance" war. "We hope it will just go away soon," he says.

"Yikes." I pull Loly down beside me and put my arm around her shoulders. "I can see why your aunt would make you feel guilty. But there isn't one single bingle thing you can do to help by not going to the concert. After it's over, we'll write letters. We'll march."

Loly shakes my arm off. "She didn't make me feel guilty. She told me, 'I went to war when I was seventeen and fought for seventeen years. It wasn't easy living in the fields, going without food, but I did it so girls like you would grow up and have fun.'"

"Well, see? I don't get it then." I am relieved. Loly's aunt will understand what a major hoo this is for both of us.

"She also told me about my mother and father, who fought beside her," Loly says in such a scratchy voice that I feel a slight twitch of panic, but I shake it away. As Mom says, nothing is ever hopeless.

"One day, my mother dropped her machine gun on the ground," Loly rushes on. "She told my aunt, 'My Kalashnikov is burning my fingers. How can we keep shooting at waves of young Ethiopian boys—boys so close I could look into their eyes?' A minute later, she was shot. Later that week, my father was also killed. My grandmother wanted to save at least me. She ran through the desert grasses for days and days saying, 'Hush, hush' when I cried. Somehow she got us to a refugee camp and to America. No wonder we never have enough money for stuff like expensive shampoo and things—she always sent most of her money back to the family left in Eritrea, and I never knew it."

My heart squeezes. I feel like a gigantic mama dinosaur. I want to schloop Loly up in my huge lizard jaws and protect her from the horrible things in the world. We will work something out because she is my very best friend who cares about my feelings, and when we get itchy-scratchy we *always* work things out.

"And what have I been doing?" Loly says in a terrible voice. "Nagging my grandmother about what shampoo I want to use. I feel so selfish."

See? I knew it. My friend does not want to be selfish. I know how to reach her. "Okay," I say gently. "Just listen to me for one minute." I tell her about how her mom would want us to do this. I tell her about Matt and about how the concert is going to change our entire lives and every cell in our brains. "All I'm asking," I say, "is for you to go with me to the concert. Then we'll figure something out about Eritrea. Can you picture how great it's going to be when I can walk across the commons like Ms. Sizzle, not a worm? Oh, Loly." I reach out to grab her hand. "You know very well it shouldn't hurt to *walk*."

Loly's face is desolate. And then, suddenly, it's full of so many other feelings I can't even name them all. But mad is in there for sure.

She jerks her hand away. "What about all those kids who won't ever in their whole lives walk again because of mines? My aunt says they piled up forty mines in her village after the Ethiopian army left there." She stands up. "I'm sorry, but you can just donate your suffering. Maybe you'll feel more *one* with those children."

Heat flames into my face. I try to say something soothing, but I choke and start to cough instead. I cannot breathe for the pain. Finally I croak, "I can't believe you said that."

Her eyes glare down into me. "And I can't believe you. People are being killed and all you can think about is your stupid concert. You—you're just an ugly American. Like the article called it a little nuisance war. You Americans treat my people like bugs. But we kneel to no one. Eritrea lives!"

She is so angry that a piece of spit flies from her mouth

and lands on my cheek. She curls her hands into fists and waves them wildly in the air as if she's about to hit me. Then she turns and walks down the sidewalk. With her go my Matt dreams and my whole sucky-yucky life.

"Wait!," I scream after her. The word ugly rings in my mind. "That is so unfair," I mutter. I yank off her friendship bracelet and throw it at her back. She doesn't pause. As I watch her, I can't stand it—I turn into a towering rage spout, spewing ugliness and not even caring. "You're just—" I yell, "just . . . an *African*. Go back to Africa, if that's all you can think about."

For one second, I consider running after her and dragging her back. I see myself reaching out—not just grabbing her but pulling her hair, choking her. I turn away, yanking my own hair because I don't know what else to do with my hands.

Sometime in my life, I will have another chance to be a wowser, and when I do, that girl is dead meat. I wish she really were a bug and I would . . . I would . . . As I think these things, I am stomping and growling up my stairs. At the top, I flimflam back and forth, howling in despair and frustration, with every single cell in my deranged young brain suddenly getting it like crazy.

Soldiers of the Stone

BY UKO BENDI UDO

KULAJA GIRI POINTED HIS HAND AT HIS HEAD AND pulled the trigger. But his hand was empty, not holding the gun he had tucked underneath his pillow. He uncoiled his fingers and sighed as beads of cold sweat marched down his dark black chest. The warm bedroom air was not the same desperate jungle air he had inhaled in his dream a few minutes ago. A nightmare. Rofurawa. More than seven thousand miles away. But he would never escape its reach.

He had been able to white out much of what had happened in the African jungle. Time would do that for you.

But the victim's face. He would never get rid of it. He instinctively looked for a cigarette, then realized Abu had seized the wilting box from him just yesterday.

He whipped the brown blanket off and rose from the squeaking bed. *Whoo-whoa! Whoo-whoa!* came the bark of the dog from a neighbor's yard close by. "*Eka-aro* to you, too," Kulaja muttered. He wondered if the dog with the big white head understood the Yoruba language.

As he walked up to the window, the smell of cooking oil caught up with him. He peeled the blind up, then jacked the glass open. Fresh air rushed in, slapping him gently on the face. He took in the moving snapshot of the powder blue sky above and the vehicles that shot along the just-visible highway. Freeway. What they called it here. The sign hanging above the asphalt read: 5 SOUTH—LOS ANGELES. NORTH—SACRAMENTO.

His gaze dropped, and that's when he noticed the scrawl on the wall. Graffiti, Abu had called such writing. But why on Abu's wall? It read FOOTHILL99.

"Kool," a voice called from behind the bedroom door. Kulaja turned. The door swung open. "You don wake?" Abu asked.

"Yes, sir," Kulaja answered. He caught himself. He was not a soldier anymore. "Yes."

"Come eat o," Abu said. At twenty-one, Abu was six years ahead of Kulaja, and he looked and acted paternal.

"I dey come," Kulaja said. "Thank you." Had Abu seen the scrawl on his wall?

The kitchen, sparse in furniture, was located on the second floor, near the living room. As Kulaja entered, Abu said to him, "Hurry, man. Your food go cold." He sat at one end of the table, which took up much of the room. Breakfast was bread, eggs, and cocoa.

"Sorry." Kulaja pulled up a chair and reached for a slice of bread from the plate. "You see that writing for your wall?"

Abu's cheeks bulged with food. "What writing?"

"You mean you no see am?" Kulaja asked.

"Where?" Abu asked, his face showing fright.

"For your wall downstairs," Kulaja said. "You can see it from my window."

Abu shot off his chair and walked toward Kulaja's room. Kulaja dropped the slice of bread on the plate and followed.

"*Olorun!*" Abu stared out the window. "That thing was not there last night when I returned."

"Who put am there?" Kulaja asked. Abu shrugged, but

the squeezing of his face suggested he knew something.

Just then a youth in a baggy outfit walked up to the wall and crouched in front of the scrawl. Abu leaned out the window and yelled, "Hey! What are you doing?" The figure flashed a brief, unconcerned look their way. He was a Mexican boy, about Kulaja's age. The hood of his gray sweat jacket covered his head. Abu turned to look at Kulaja. "I don't believe this!"

"Who is he?"

"A neighbor." Abu leaned out of the window again. "Hey, boy! What are you doing?" The boy ignored Abu as he sprayed the word Looniz above the initial scrawl. Abu broke away from the window and hurried out of the room. Kulaja followed. In the living room, Abu put on his leather jacket. He turned the radio and TV off. "I dey come," Abu said.

Kulaja moved forward. Abu waved him back. "Stay. Let me handle this." His shoes made thumping noises as he descended the staircase. Kulaja walked back to the window in his room.

Below him, Abu approached the boy, who had now drawn a big X where the FOOTHILL99 sign was. The boy stood up, sprayed Abu with the paint, flung the can angrily against the wall, and swaggered away. Kulaja's eyes narrowed. He walked into his closet and grabbed a jacket.

Should he get the gun stashed under the pillow? His senses were battle ready. He was back in the jungle. A soldier. Ready to defend the honor of his platoon.

He heard the door downstairs open and slam shut. He put on the jacket. By the time he got out of his room, Abu was nowhere to be seen. Kulaja ran down the staircase. As he opened the door, he could feel his military juices percolate. The first thing he was going to do was make the fool kneel down and beg for his life.

"Kool!"

Kulaja stopped.

"Kulaja. Where you dey go?"

Kulaja looked up. Abu was leaning out of the window in Kulaja's room.

Kulaja's mind was in a riot. "Never be a soldier of the stone. Never invest in the stone," Iyawa, the head wife in his family, had told him. Was he about to invest?

"Come back up here!" Abu ordered.

Kulaja's heart was heaving.

"Kulaja, come back up. *Now!*" They always reverted to mainstream English whenever they were serious. Kulaja reversed his steps. He could feel his nerves quiet down as he made his way upstairs, using the calming technique that the U.S. doctor had taught him. Inhale deeply. Get his mind away from the battlefields of Sierra Leone's civil war.

Abu met him at the door of his room. "Wetin be this?" He had Kulaja's gun in his hand. His face was twisted like a wet towel.

"A gun." Kulaja's voice was matter-of-fact.

"What is it doing in my house?"

"I have to have it."

"For what?"

"Protection."

"Protection from what?"

Kulaja shrugged his shoulders. "When you are in Rome, do like the Romans."

Abu's eyes narrowed like he was listening to a foreign language. "Who told you this is Rome? Does this look like Rome to you, eh?"

"When you are in the jungle, act like it." Kulaja's jaw tightened.

Abu led the way back to the kitchen. "Sit down!" He stormed away.

Kulaja threw the breathing technique out the window. He reached out and slapped the plastic plates off the table, splattering the kitchen divider with food and beverage. Calm down, he admonished himself. He quickly rose up and cleared as much of the mess as he could. Should he be angry at himself for not putting the gun away, or at Abu for allowing that boy to disrespect him?

Abu came back into the room without the gun. He surveyed the mess on the floor, then sat down. He waved at Kulaja to sit, too. "Where did you get the gun?"

"Around here." Kulaja's right leg quivered impatiently under the table.

"Around where?"

"On the street."

"From whom?"

"From the street."

"I don't know of anyone called The Street. How much did you pay for it?"

"Fifty dollars?"

"You have that kind of money to waste?"

Kulaja sucked in air. "I need it."

Abu slammed the table with his fist. "No, you do not need it, Kulaja! You need that gun like you need poison for breakfast!" As Abu paced the floor, Kulaja began to feel better. Maybe Abu would transfer that energy into anger toward that boy.

"I did not like what the boy did," Kulaja said.

"Well, I do not like it, either!"

Kulaja looked up at him. "Then do something about it!"

Abu's steely surface cracked. He rubbed his temples as he paced. "It's not as easy as you think."

"Then let me go teach him a lesson!" Kulaja stood up.

"Yes." Abu nodded derisively. "Just like you taught those poor kids in Sierra Leone a lesson. How does cutting off a child's hand teach him a lesson?"

Kulaja slumped back into his chair. "I did not cut anybody's hand," he said softly. He could feel Rofurawa coming back.

"Then where were you when your fellow . . . *thugs* were doing it? Where were you?"

Kulaja took in a deep breath. The victim's face flashed in his mind again. She pleaded for her life. He took a step back. The gun exploded. Her head snapped backward. She was gurgling, twitching, twitching. Like the fowl that's just lost its head for dinner's sake.

"What sort of people would do such a thing?" Abu's anger seemed aimed at something else. Something distant. "*Savages!*" He said it with such force spit shot out of his mouth. He pointed toward the east. "That's where the jungle is. The whole lousy continent is a jungle!"

210

So Abu had some bitter juice in him, too?

"That's why I got out!" Abu leaned toward Kulaja. "That's why I am *here*!" He slumped onto the chair, exhausted, as if he had just regurgitated a bone that had been stuck in his throat for a long time. They sat in silence. Then Abu stood up and left the room.

Kulaja looked for the broom. He swept up more of his mess. Back in his room, he gazed out at the scrawl. Just then a big car crawled into the driveway of the house. Behind the wheel was a Mexican lady. When she got out, Kulaja left his room to go open the door, but then he heard Abu's footsteps on the stairs. The doorbell chimed.

"Hi," the woman's voice said. "That graffiti is really stupid. Did you see the kid?"

Rosa. The voice on the phone. Abu's girlfriend.

"Yes," Abu said. "He got angry when I confronted him."

Rosa was the one who had helped Abu buy the house. Abu had said she was into selling houses. She'd been on a trip for two or three weeks.

The door closed. "He sprayed my jacket," Abu said.

"These kids are impossible! Did you call the cops?"

"Yes. As usual they gave me the runaround and told me to call another city department."

"Where's your brother?"

"Kulaja!" Abu called. Kulaja listened to the footsteps. Rosa appeared at the top of the staircase. Her bright smile sucked Kulaja in, then she covered him with a long, warm hug.

"Welcome to Los Angeles!" she said. "How are you?" She took off her breaker and hung it on a chair. "Have you had breakfast?" She saw the remaining mess on the floor and tiptoed around it. "What happened here?"

Kulaja tried to pick up some of the bread crumbs.

"Leave it alone," she said. "Abu!"

Abu showed up in the kitchen wearing a new shirt. "Honey, can you go get some groceries so we can make a proper breakfast for Kool?" Rosa turned to Kulaja. "We don't have *ogi* here, but some plantain and eggs will do, right?"

How did she know about *ogi*, the popular Nigerian breakfast staple? He loved this lady already.

Two hours later, Kulaja was smelling the best breakfast he had tasted since he left Nigeria. He and Rosa sat at the table eating from glass plates full of fried plantains, eggs, and potatoes. She also had some other things on her plate. Mexican delicacies. Abu had decided not to wait for the city and was getting some paint so he could cover the scrawl.

"What other Nigerian foods have you tried?" Kulaja asked.

"Actually, Mexicans eat plantain, too," Rosa said. Kulaja arched a brow. "And goat!"

Kulaja almost jumped out of his seat. "You do?"

"Matter of fact, Abu and I plan on going to this place where we can get some goat," Rosa said.

Kulaja smiled. "I like goat meat."

"I know," Rosa said. "Abu told me."

What else had Abu told her about him? "Where did you learn to fry plantain like this?" Kulaja asked.

"Guess."

Kulaja silently guessed. Abu. Rosa rose from her chair, washed an apple, sliced up the fruit, and brought the pieces back to the table. "Abu tells me that you two don't share a mother."

"We share the same father," Kulaja said. "His mother is the first wife in my family."

"*First* wife?"

"My father had many wives."

Curiosity colored her face. "How many?"

"Twenty."

She dropped her food and allowed her mouth to hang open for a second. "Twenty?" she said, almost in a whisper.

"Yes." He was eating more than he had eaten since he'd arrived in the country. And he was talking more, too. Maybe too much.

"Abu never told me this," Rosa said. "How did you like being in that . . . situation?"

"I did not care. But my mother did not like it." Kulaja drank some of the 7Up in the glass in front of him. It burned his tongue deliciously. "She moved us to Sierra Leone." Kulaja stopped. Dangerous territory.

"Abu told me about that," Rosa said. "Was your mother from Sierra Leone?"

"And our father."

"Abu said your dad passed away in Nigeria," Rosa said.

"Yes," Kulaja said.

"Where is your mother?"

Kulaja took his time. The sad juice inside of him started to rise. "We don't know."

"Sorry."

For what? Kulaja thought. You did not do anything to her. He waited, then asked, "What did Abu tell you?"

"That you were in the army over there."

Maybe Abu was the one who talked too much. "I was."

Her face asked the follow-up question. "I did not choose to go into it." Kulaja wanted to stop. "They kidnapped me." He swallowed hard. He dropped his fork and leaned back against the chair. "They taught me how to shoot the gun . . . how to kill." He looked away. "And I killed." Tears began to run down his face. "Many people." He began a slow, gentle sob. "Many people." He let it come. Opened the gate. Cried like he had wanted to for a long time. Wasn't it funny that he was doing it in front of this stranger whom he barely knew? She offered her shoulders and he took them, remembering his mother.

Later in the day, after Abu and Rosa had gone goat hunting, Kulaja sat by the window in his room. For the first time in a long time he felt . . . good. He had told Rosa not to tell Abu about the episode. That would be a test. If Abu ever mentioned it, that would mean she had told him. So far, he liked her. What else did Nigerians share with Mexicans? Certainly not looks.

Just then he saw a hooded figure swaggering past the house. Wasn't that the Mexican boy that had spray-painted Abu's wall? Kulaja came off the chair. He reached under the pillow for his gun. Wait—Abu had taken it. He put on his jacket.

Outside, he looked down the street. The hooded figure entered the second house on the left side. Kulaja cautiously moved toward the building. The sidewalk was awash with October leaves cut off from their big and sturdy mother trees. From its look, this was not a bad neighborhood. But he could see graffiti, like Abu called it.

When Kulaja reached the front of the house, he stopped. It was a one-story cream-colored house with blue trimmings. Rap music was coming from somewhere. A black doorbell button jutted out of the wall. Should he ring it?

What should he say to the boy? He did not know, which was not necessarily a bad thing. His military juices were flowing, but not like they had been earlier today. This time he was calmer. Better prepared, he thought. He pressed the doorbell. No movement behind the door. He pressed it again. No answer. "Hello," he called out. Nothing.

Calmly he walked toward the gate that led into the backyard. As he opened it, he saw the hooded figure— hunched under the raised hood of a car, working on the engine. Music boomed from the car's opened trunk. It was definitely the same boy who had spray-painted Abu's wall this morning. A few feet away, chained to a tree, was the dog with the big white head. The dog noticed Kulaja, jumped to its feet, and began barking, *Whoo-whoa!* The strange bark had something in it that sounded like a human inflection.

The boy jumped, dropping a tool that clanged its way down the car's engine. After a quick glance at Kulaja, he dashed to the tree, working to unleash the lunging, barking dog. By the time the animal came off its leash, Kulaja was already running, his military senses sharp and taut. He caught a surprised look on the boy's face as Kulaja raced *toward* him instead of away. But Kulaja was aiming for the car.

Please let both front doors, at least the driver's door, be unlocked, Kulaja thought. He could feel the barking beast almost at his heels as he flung open the driver-side door—*good*—and dove into the car, feet first, leaving the door open. He tugged the passenger-side door handle toward him, knowing from the dog's howls that it was right behind him. The door flew open. He tumbled out and slammed the door shut, locking it. Furious, the dog attacked the passenger-side window, ignoring the escape route behind.

Kulaja slammed the raised hood of the vehicle down and jumped on top of it. The dog lunged for the windshield, ramming his oversized pit-bull head against it as he barked. He cocked his head to the side to reveal scary fangs that dripped foamy dog spit. Kulaja reached around and kicked the driver-side door shut, locking the dog in completely. But before he could celebrate, the boy was in his face, waving a gun, directing Kulaja to get off the car. Kulaja obeyed, still suppressing any hint of fear.

"Shuddup!" the boy barked at the dog. Then he turned to Kulaja. "Who you, homes? What set you from?" The dog whimpered for a second, then resumed its barking.

Set? Homes? What was this talk? "My name is Kulaja and I live at the house you scrawled something on this morning."

The boy's demeanor softened a little bit. "Man, you have the nerve! You trespassed my property and then tell me I did somn'? I should blow you 'way, man!"

Right. This was not Sierra Leone or Nigeria. Abu had warned him. You couldn't just walk onto anyone's property like back home. "I came in peace," Kulaja said, raising his hands. "I wanted to talk."

"'Bout what?"

"The scrawl."

"*Scrawl?*" the boy said derisively.

"Graffiti," Kulaja said.

The boy's eyes narrowed. "Graffiti?" He repeated it like Kulaja had just insulted him. "Whataboutit, homes?"

"I'd like for you to clean it off," Kulaja said.

"Clean it off?" The boy sucked air loudly. "You must have a death wish, man. I can do you the favor right now!" The dog barked a little harder. "Shuddup, Bugz!" the boy yelled.

"I don't think my brother's house deserved to be . . . marked like that," Kulaja said.

"Fools chose your house, man. Thought it was mine. *Your* problem, man!"

"Who are these fools?"

"Fools, man!" The boy licked his dry lips. "Looking for trouble, that's all. Where you from?"

"Sierra Leone."

"Siya what?" the boy said.

"Sierra Leone," Kulaja said. "Africa."

"Why don't you go back there before you get killed, homes?" The boy lowered the gun.

"What's your name?" Kulaja asked.

"Angel of Death, homes." He swallowed hard as he studied Kulaja. "Get off my property, man, before I hurt you."

"My name is Kulaja."

Angel of Death's response was a scowl. Kulaja turned around and started walking. By the time he reached the gate, he heard the car door open. He slipped behind the gate just as Bugz got to it, flashing his famous fangs.

As Kulaja walked back toward Abu's house, he knew exactly what he was going to do next. He was going to get the paint. From Angel of Death's reaction earlier, painting over the graffiti was a risk. But a statement had to be made. This was Abu's property. And only he could paint a graffiti on it. Full stop. Or period, like they said here.

The next day Kulaja woke up early to see if the graffiti had been spray-painted back on the wall. It hadn't. He had another reason to celebrate. His nightmare had not been as severe, either. After Abu left for work, Kulaja went downstairs to the entertainment room and turned on the big-screen TV. An English soccer match was being telecast on Fox Sports World. Just after he settled down to watch it, the doorbell rang. This early? At the front door he looked through the peephole. Angel of Death was the visitor. Open the door or not? He chose to open it. "Hello," Kulaja said cheerfully. "How are you, Angel of Death?"

"Sup," Angel of Death said. "Marco." His gaze was fixated on an object behind Kulaja. Kulaja looked. The TV.

"Your name is Marco?"

"Marco," Marco muttered. He kept looking past Kulaja. "Shouldn'ta done it, man."

"Done what?"

"Wipe my tag," Marco said. He sucked in air. "Told you not to do it."

"I'm sorry, but you didn't," Kulaja said.

Marco cocked his head. "Didn't?"

Kulaja shook his head no. "Why don't you come in, Marco?" Kulaja opened the iron screen door and stepped aside.

Marco guardedly walked into the house. "Who was the dude I made my point to yesterday?"

"My brother, Abu," Kulaja said. "Can I offer you something, Marco?"

Marco shook his head no. "He from Africa, too? Bubu?"

"Abu," Kulaja corrected. "Yes." He turned down the TV volume.

"You guys talk funny, man," Marco said.

"Thanks." Far from it, Kulaja thought. He could not remember saying anything funny in a long, long time.

"You guys like soccer?" Marco walked up to the big couch facing the TV and sat in it.

"I used to play it when I was in Sierra Leone." Kulaja's voice trailed off at the end of the sentence. He sucked in air to banish the flashback. "Do you play it?"

Marco shrugged no. "Not anymore. Back in Mexico I did."

Kulaja noticed that Marco's voice trailed off at the end, too. Why was he really here? To shoot him? Kulaja brushed the thought off. He was not afraid to die, if it came to that. It would be something he was not unprepared for.

"You ditched school, man?" Marco asked.

Ditched?

"Why're you not in school?" Marco asked again.

Was he here to play father? "I will be starting next month."

"Where?"

"Verdugo Hill," Kulaja said.

"Why? Schools around here not good enough for you?" Marco smiled.

The first time he'd made a stab at humor. Maybe *he* was the funny one. "My brother chose the school. Not me. Who do you stay with, Marco?"

"Grams."

"Grams?"

"Grandmother." They were quiet for a while, watching

222

the soccer game on TV. "How is high school in Africa?" Marco asked.

"I never went to high school in Africa."

That distracted Marco. "What'd you do, man?"

Kulaja took his time. "I was a soldier." From the corner of his eye, Kulaja saw Marco lean forward on the couch.

"Soldier?"

Kulaja nodded yes.

"For real?" Marco said.

For real? Kulaja wondered. Then he understood. "Yes. And I killed a lot of people. And it was not worth it." Kulaja was surprised at his calmness.

"Who you fightin'?"

Kulaja hesitated. "The government."

"Your government in Africa? Why?"

"It was corrupt."

"You were in the rebel army?" Marco asked.

Kulaja nodded yes. He wondered if Marco knew more than he let on.

"How old are you, man?" Marco asked.

"Your age."

"How old you think I am?"

"Fifteen."

"Now I know why," Marco said.

"Why what?"

"Yesterday, man." There was a glint of admiration in Marco's eyes. "Bugz couldn't believe he didn't get you, man!"

Bugz? Excited? He *talked* to his dog?

"That was bad, man! I mean, I was sayin' what *set* he with, man!" Marco rose to his feet and began reenacting scenes from Kulaja's performance with the dog. "I said I wanna join his set! Where'd you learn that, man?" Marco jumped around, chopped the air, and performed a few martial-arts moves of his own creation. The gun fell out of his pocket and landed at Kulaja's foot. Marco stopped. Kulaja picked up the gun and handed it back to him. Marco accepted it and then sat down. Suddenly he looked somber. They both sat still for a few minutes, silent. Then Marco spoke. "My father was a rebel fighter, too."

That caught Kulaja's ears. "Which army?"

"Chiapas."

"Where is that?"

"Mexico. Yeah. He was fightin' for the poor Indians, man." Marco smiled. But the smile looked eerily familiar. It was a sad smile. A hurting smile. "Yeah. He died for the poor Indians, man!"

"He was not a soldier of the stone," Kulaja said. "That's

what my stepmother in Nigeria calls those that die fighting for vain causes. Seems your father died fighting for a good cause." Suddenly the TV did not matter anymore. "I was a soldier of the stone," Kulaja continued. "I started off fighting for the cause of the people. Fighting for a just Sierra Leone." He sucked in air. "I ended up fighting for stones. Diamonds. Stones that would end up making us do things to each other our worst enemies wouldn't do to us." Kulaja sucked in air. He took a look at Marco. The boy's gaze was distant, but then focused again. For the first time he leaned back on the couch and really relaxed.

"I want to be like my father," Marco said. Kulaja looked. Marco had spoken mainstream English. "I don't want to be a soldier of the stone." Kulaja leaned forward, then rested back on the couch, a smile on his face.

"You are a soldier of the stone if a graffiti on a piece of stone matters more to you than the people that live inside that stone," Kulaja said.

The silence after that was long and deep. The TV noise did not matter.

Suddenly Marco's relaxed demeanor hardened back up again. "Looniz for life!" Marco said. "That's the way it has to be here in the 'hood, man." He shot off the couch and ran out of the house.

225

Kulaja sat for a long time feeling . . . light inside. Yesterday he had almost been a soldier of the stone. Ready to take a life or give his because of a scrawl on a stone. But today he had spoken with the real Marco. The one forced to live behind the Angel of Death. The thought made him feel powerful. Maybe there was some reason he must live, in spite of all the bad things he'd done up to this point in his life. He walked over and locked the front door, all the while smiling.

Lying Down with the Lion

BY SONIA LEVITIN

THEY TELL HIM THAT SOON THE GROUND WILL BE hard, frozen. Trees will lose their leaves; only brown sticks will remain. Birds will grow silent, most of them having flown away to a warmer place. Ajang tries to imagine the change, as once he knew changing from dry season to wet, with creatures hatching and braying, crawling out upon the earth to sing out their joy of life.

Ajang knows some joy now, too. He knows the joy of understanding how to reach the trolley that takes him to the school and of no longer fearing its roar. He knows the joy of hearing the other boys shout and laugh, and the feeling of their hands on his back and shoulders because he has run the lap in "no-time."

They have this strange idea of "no-time," telling him, "Just down the street, there, you can buy meat from the small cart, a hot dog—you'll be there in no-time."

He is learning their metaphor. No-time means little-time. He has learned that hot dog is not an animal at all, but something he can quickly chew and pay for with only a few coins. He has learned much since first arriving. He and his two friends, Wol and Ngor, were taken to a strange stack of huts, one on top of the other, and small platforms where they could stand, but from which they must never climb. The woman with the speckled face called it a balcony, and she charged Wol and Ngor to look after Ajang, for they were men already, finished with school except to go night times for English lessons and to learn about a constitution and rules. There were so many rules. When the woman with the speckled face came to teach them, she wagged her finger and spoke of many things they must not do. She showed them the cage that lifts people up and brings them down again, and then she wagged her finger once more and said, "Only when you must! You may not ride up and down all day—no, it is only for necessity. Do you understand? For necessity."

For necessity, also, was the cold box that shivered in the room with the water pipes, where his friends Wol and Ngor put their extra clothes, filling it up. When the speckle-faced woman saw what they had done, she wagged her finger once again, then turned away, and her shoulders shook vigorously. "It is for food," she said. "For food, to keep it fresh. Your clothes belong here, in the closet." Ajang knew, from her eyes, that she had been laughing. He loved this laughter, though it puzzled him.

At first only Ajang went to buy food. He was the one who best knew the English, for he had gone to the missionary school in Khartoum. He went long enough to learn how to wear shoes, how to read and write, and about such wonders as the god who was killed and rose up again. When Ajang told stories of his people, his ancestors, of the lion and hippopotamus and the cobra, and the things that God had said, they did not believe him. Then the Old Robed Ones scolded and threatened to punish him, to send him home to his father, Chief Kir Nyong, in disgrace.

But it is hard to live without stories. Ajang tells his stories to himself at night. He writes them on the yellow pad, using a sharp pencil. He does not like to write them into the computer, which eats them up sometimes. Ajang tells stories to Wol and Ngor, but often they fall asleep while he is speaking. When Ajang sits at his desk at night, he can see into the window of another place. He can hear the voices of the people—man and woman, two boys and a small girl. Sometimes he even hears words.

" . . . why not? Doesn't he go to your school? You said he is in your social studies class."

"Yeah, well—lots of guys go to my school and we don't have them over for dinner."

"But it is the decent thing to do. The neighborly thing . . . it would be a kindness to show him . . . "

Strange, that he is given to hear these words. Or maybe he only thinks he heard them, as sometimes things do not follow one another in exact order, and the mind later rearranges them to make a better story. In the morning the boy, Terry, is running from his house to the trolley, and Ajang runs, too. Terry climbs up the steps, panting. He stands close to Ajang and says, "Hey, will you come to our house for dinner Friday night? My parents said I should ask you."

Ajang is frowning. Perhaps he ought to smile. It is very difficult to figure out which is best, and hard to pull his face from one expression to the other. In Sudan, to accept an invitation too eagerly is to lose dignity, as if one were

Ajang reaches into his pocket. Some bills lie there, wages from his job on Saturdays, when he cleans and prepares the sports track at the elementary school and also teaches the boys how to run.

"I will go to the department store," Ajang says, licking his lips.

He has been to the department store once before. Its confusions of sounds and smells left him feeling dizzy and ill, so that the hot dog he had eaten for lunch came halfway up his chest again.

Now he walks past the counter, where a young woman with sleek hair and a very white face smiles at him brightly. "Are you looking for a gift?" she says.

Ajang licks his lips, nodding. "Yes, a gift."

"For a lady?"

He nods. Yes, he must bring a gift for the mother of Terry who is providing the meal.

The girl shows him small boxes with powders of many colors—blue, green, purple, and brown. "It is for her eyes," the girl says, smiling. "The women all love this."

Ajang gives her many coins and paper monies—twelve dollars altogether—and he puts the gift in his pocket, secure in the small white sack the girl gave him. His friends Wol and Ngor are highly pleased with Ajang's purchase. All of them wait for Friday, when Ajang will find himself in the house of the neighbor who has sought to honor him with this invitation.

Ajang wears his freshly laundered pants and a shirt that belongs to Wol, blue with tan figures printed on it, shapes of leaves and fishes. It is a fine shirt, hanging out over his pants, and he wears running shoes and, of course, the large watch on his wrist.

He waits until it is exactly two minutes before seven, and then he takes the cage downstairs, goes out one door and in another, to the other cage, which he rides until he comes to the sixth floor. He wonders, as he rides, whether from this place he will be able to look into his own room, as from his room he can see into theirs. He wonders with a laugh what it might be like to see his own self sitting there! It would make a good story, he thinks, and he plans to write this later tonight.

He rings the doorbell and is greatly pleased with the sound of it—a chime. In a moment the door is pulled open, and there stands the father, eye to eye with Ajang, a thin man with graying hair. Behind him is the woman, wearing jeans and a creased, round face. Then come the children, Terry and two more.

"Hello! Come in. Ajang, is it? Terry told us you have some classes together. This is my other boy, Matthew, and our daughter, Kimberly. Come in! Come in! Terry tells us you are a terrific runner. Do you also play basketball?"

And so it goes, the questions and Ajang's answers, while all around the table there are smiles and little coos and oohs and nods whenever Ajang speaks. The mother brings food and everyone eats, speaking while they are eating, not stopping to chew, and Ajang eats two and three times from the soft, white, foaming potatoes and twice from the roasted meat that is lamb, together with a green sweet sauce.

"You like lamb," says the mother.

"Very much. It is all delicious," Ajang says.

The mother and father and all the children look very pleased. It is a good thing they have done, to give this stranger some food.

"And who cooks for you boys at your place?" asks the mother.

"We all cook bits," Ajang says. "My best is spinach and corn. Wol cooks cereal. Ngor—well, he goes to the market and buys food. Sometimes a chicken in a box."

The father laughs. "I suppose, in Sudan, you never saw a chicken in a box."

"Our chickens played in front of the huts," Ajang says, "until they gave us their lives."

"Gave you their lives?" asks the girl, Kimberly. "You mean, they wanted to die?"

"We believe there is a place for animals in the world," says Ajang, "and that all know their place. It is given by God. We have many stories about animals, you see, and so we learn the truth."

"You believe in God!" cries the young boy, Matthew. "I thought you were pagans!"

"That's enough," says the father in a stern voice. Ajang has heard the father and Terry in argument, loud sometimes, and he has pondered the strange war that often lies just beneath the surface between a father and his son.

The mother tries to make peace, saying, "Maybe Ajang will tell us one of his stories."

Terry turns his eyes up to the ceiling. He slides around in his chair, looks at the time on his wrist. His mouth makes some words without sound.

His father gives him a harsh glance, points down. The little girl begins to twist her hair around her two fingers.

"We would love to hear a story," says the father. He pours himself another cup of tea, stirs in two squares of sugar. "Please."

236

Ajang looks from face to face. How many, many nights he has lain in his hut, being put to sleep by the storyteller! How many days in the cattle camp, fat from creamy milk and joyful from dancing, has he sat with his friends while stories were woven all around them, the voice of the teller mingling with the bells and the groans from the cattle, and the full moon looked down and smiled or wept at the tales.

Ajang sighs and begins, as all storytellers do: "This is an ancient event. Once there was a man, a great chief, who had a son much beloved. The chief took care to teach his son everything he knew. Every day, when the chief was sitting under the tree, speaking wisdom to the people, his son sat beside him, hearing how his father settled matters between man and man, man and woman, or jealousies of women together."

Here Terry's mother smiles and nods to her girl.

"All the people praised their chief, and soon his son began also to speak wisdom, deciding that a cow should be paid in return for an insult, or what bride price for a girl who was lame, or how two brothers might stop their quarrel by building a road between their huts."

Ajang looks around the table at the faces; nobody has moved. They listen well, like Dinka children, only these people are white and speckled. No matter—a story is a story, and a good listener is always a friend.

"Well, the day came," Ajang continues, "that the son desired to go on a journey to see the great chief of the land near the mountains, for travelers had brought word of this man's holiness and his wisdom.

"'No!' said the boy's father. 'I will not let you risk the dangers of such a journey. You are already a wise young man; may you grow to be great, as great as your ancestors, from whom you are descended.'

"But the boy begged and begged to go on the journey to speak with this holy and wise chief. The boy's longing made him sad and weak, and at last the father said, 'Very well. You may go to find the great holy chief, and I shall go with you. But let us agree that if something bad happens on the road, we will take it as a sign from God, and we will return home to our village.'

"Of course the boy agreed, so happy was he to be going."

It seems to Ajang that Terry is looking long and hard at his father, a look that tells of knowing such feelings, too. Ajang continues. "The father and son set out, and they walked and walked for two days, when, lo! It began to rain a terrible storm that laid out a flood at their very feet, and yet it was not the season for such a thing. 'It is a sign,' said the father. 'We must return home to our village and give up this foolish quest.'

"So they returned," says Ajang. "But you know how it is." He steals a glance at Terry, another at Matthew, knowing that the parents are listening, hoping for the wisdom that a story might give. "After a time, the boy again began to beg and cry to go on the journey, to speak with the great, holy chief. So much did the boy yearn that he did not sleep but cried out in the night, and the father could not bear it. So once again he agreed that they would make the journey together. 'But if we encounter any evil thing on the way,' the father said, 'that will be a sign to us that we must return to our village and give up this foolish quest.'

"So the father and the boy set out once again, and after they had walked for three days, there in the middle of the road was a crocodile, looking fierce and hungry. The great beast stretched its mouth wide, jaws snapping open and shut. The father pulled his son by the arm, and they ran and did not stop running until they were home again in their hut.

"Time passed. And once again the boy began to beg and weep for his desire. So strong was his need that he could not eat, and he became thin and weak, and his father was very afraid. So once more he agreed that they would make the journey together. This time there was no talk of what evil might befall them, for both knew it would be their last attempt. A third effort is noble; a fourth is foolishness."

Ajang feels the expectant mood of his listeners. He continues. "Father and son set out once again, and they walked until night was approaching. And there before them on the road, having sprung out from behind a bush, stood a huge, fierce lion. With a single leap and a roar, the lion was upon the boy, and in one gulp, ate him.

"Oh, the cries from the father! He beat his chest and tore his hair in grief. 'My son! Give me back my son!' he cried. In his agony, the father grasped the lion by the tail, holding tight, so tight that the lion, as much as he whipped himself around, could not get free. 'Give me back my son,' shouted the father, 'or I will cut off your tail!'

"'Cut my tail if you must,' answered the lion, 'but I will never return your son.'

"With that, the father sliced off the lion's tail. The lion roared in pain. Then he stretched out on the road and spoke. 'Lie down with me, for I am your kin, and your protector. You will have another son,' said the lion, 'and when he wishes to seek wisdom, you will let him go. You will make a standard of my tail, and keep it with you always, to remind you that a father's love cannot exist where there is pride, nor can a young man grow when the father wants to keep him small.'

"'How dare you say these things to me!' cried the father. 'It was not pride that made me keep my son from wandering. We saw signs from heaven, first a flood, then a crocodile, warning us to end this useless quest!'

"The lion shook his great mane and said, 'The flood you saw was but a river, sent by God to move you swiftly on your way. The crocodile was in truth a kindly beast, desiring to carry you in its jaws so you would arrive safely at your destination. You called them evil signs because of your fear and your pride. You would not let your son go on to become greater than you. Now lie down with me, for we are kin, and I tell you true things, to help you on your way.'"

Ajang feels himself breathing heavily, his face so hot, as if he were sitting by the campfire in the cattle camp, telling this tale.

"What happened then?" asks the girl, Kimberly. And Matthew asks, "Did the chief have another son? And did he let him go?"

Ajang smiles. "What do you think?" he says. "A story is a good story when the listeners decide its meaning and its end."

Now it is growing late. Everyone stands up, signaling that it is time for Ajang to take the small cage back down and up again, to go home.

Before he goes, Ajang reaches into his pocket and brings out the gift. The mother's eyes widen in surprise. Ajang watches her open the small package. He sees that her eyes are pale, without colors around them. He has given her exactly what she needs, what every woman wants, as the girl in the store has told him.

"Thank you, Ajang," the mother whispers. She smiles. "Thank you."

So Ajang goes home, feeling his dignity has been raised high, and so happy that he sleeps without writing another story. He sleeps well, very well.

The next school day, as Ajang runs for the trolley, he hears Terry shouting, "Wait! Ajang, wait for me!"

They climb up onto the car, standing close together. Terry is excited, smiling and gasping from pleasure. He takes Ajang's arm, pulls him close. Ajang feels the heat of the boy's body and smells his smell, somewhat like milk. "I'm going to spend the summer with my uncle in

Florida, crewing on his boat!" Terry cries out, and several passengers look over at the two boys. "Do you realize what you did for me? That story—"

"You want to work at sea?" asks Ajang. "On a boat?" The idea is so strange to him, but his friend's face is shining.

"I love boats, everything about them!" says Terry. "My uncle invited me to work with him, but my father always gave reasons not to let me go, excuses—he was in the navy, you know. He was always telling me about the navy and his experiences, and I think . . . " Terry stops. He is grinning.

"I think he is lying down now with the lion," says Ajang. "Well, it is a good story. I am glad, my friend, that you will go on your quest."

About the Authors

MONICA ARAC DE NYEKO was born, raised, and still lives in Uganda. She studied literature and English language studies at Makerere University and is a teacher of literature at St. Mary's College Kisubi (SMACK). Her short fiction and poetry have been published in *Words from a Granary, Tears of Hope, Wordwrite,* and the Berlin poetry anthology. Her poetry is forthcoming with Poetry International and her novella *The Last Dance* is forthcoming from Fountain Publishers. She is a fellow on Crossing Borders, a British Council-funded creative writer's course. She enjoys playing volleyball.

She says, "I have always been touched by how the choices parents make affect their children. When I was young, we lived next door to a child whose mother had been unfaithful to her husband with her husband's brother. It was horrible for the child after the couple decided to keep their marriage together. This one child had to live with being disliked by everybody. His mother saw the child as someone who messed up her marriage. His mother's husband saw him as an ugly reminder of his wife's infidelity. His real father saw him as the child who should never have been born. All of these sad realities came down upon the innocent boy, who did not have a choice in all of it. When something like this troubles me, I seem to want to write about it."

SELAMAWI "MAWI" ASGEDOM graduated from Harvard University as one of eight Harvard Marshals and delivered the graduation speech in 1999 to a crowd of thirty thousand. Since then he has worked as a professional speaker and inspired more than one hundred thousand people all across America. He published his first book, *Of Beetles and Angels: A Boy's Journey from a Refugee Camp to Harvard* to major critical acclaim. His second book, *The Code: The 5 Secrets of Teen Success*, will be released in Fall

2003. Mawi has been featured on *Oprah* and in the *Chicago Tribune* and other national media. In 2002 he was selected for *Essence* magazine's prestigious list of "Forty of the Most Inspiring African-Americans." He now lives in Chicago, where he enjoys playing basketball and spending time with friends and family. He can be reached at *www.mawispeaks.com*.

He says, "I fled war-torn Ethiopia at age three. My family lived in a Sudanese refugee camp for three years before emigrating to the United States in 1983. Growing up in America, I struggled with welfare, personal tragedy, and cultural challenges before earning a full-tuition scholarship to Harvard University. 'My Brother's Heart' shares my brother Tewolde's amazing spirit, and is adapted from my first book, *Of Beetles and Angels: A Boy's Journey from a Refugee Camp to Harvard*."

ELANA BREGIN is a Durban-based author, currently working as a freelance writer, editor, and lecturer. The Bushmen are her area of special interest and her thesis was entitled "The Identity of Difference: A Critical Study of Representations of the Bushmen." As an author, she is well-known for her award-winning young adult titles, such as *The Red-Haired Khumalo, The Boy from the Other Side*, and *The Kayaboeties*, which focus on South African sociopolitical themes. *The Slayer of Shadows*, a magic realist novel for older readers, was awarded the English Academy's Percy FitzPatrick Prize for Youth Literature in 2000. She also has had several children's stories published in the U.K., including *The Magical Bicycle, A School for Amos*, and "Now We Are Free," which forms part of the prestigious Amnesty International *Dare to be Different* collection.

"As a white South African who grew up under apartheid, I have had to travel a long road in order to be able to claim my place as a woman not just *in* Africa, but *of* Africa. I love being part of this unique continent, with all its problems. I love its harshness and beauty and challenge and incredible richness of spirit. I cannot imagine being happy anywhere else. 'Ella's Dunes' is about many issues that are close to my heart: the survival struggles of the Cape Kalahari Bushmen, caught between spiritual needs and material demands; the difficulties of being different in a world that doesn't allow for the value of difference; our need to first cross personal boundaries in ourselves and take a journey of the spirit before we can find our connection with others; and the realization that our true family, those we feel our deepest sense of belonging with, are sometimes not the peer group or tribe we were born into."

LINDSEY CLARK spent a quiet childhood in a suburb of Milwaukee, Wisconsin. After studying for a year in Padova, Italy, and graduating from Wellesley College in 1999, she joined Teach For America and taught science to sixth graders in rural North Carolina for two years. She served as a Peace Corps volunteer in northern Morocco from 2002 to 2003. Except for work in *Aeolus*, Wellesley College's literary magazine, this is her first published poem.

"'Into the Maghreb' grew out of my experiences living and working with the people of a small Arab village in the foothills of the Rif Mountains, near the city of Taza. While struggling to learn Moroccan Arabic, I was helping the local farmer's association pursue projects such as bringing solar energy to the village. I spent much of my time learning and thinking about Moroccan culture and the complexities of being an American in Morocco. Nothing short of a book could tackle that subject, but I was continually amazed and grateful for the unconditional hospitality of my Moroccan friends, and I hope that this piece communicates some of what a first-time visitor to the country might experience."

MERI NANA-AMA DANQUAH is the author of *Willow Weep for Me: A Black Woman's Journey through Depression*, which was hailed by the *Washington Post* as "a vividly textured flower of a memoir which will surely stand as one of the finest to come along in years." She is the editor of *Becoming American: Personal Essays by First-Generation Immigrant Women* and *Shaking the Tree: A Collection of New Fiction and Memoir by Black Women*. The recipient of a California Arts Council individual artist fellowship in creative nonfiction, Ms. Danquah is currently at work on *Aby's America*, a young-adult novel about immigration, which will be published in 2004 by Orchard Books. She lives in Washington, D.C., with her daughter.

"I was born in Ghana, where I lived for six years before moving with my family to the United States. I belong to the class of immigrants often referred to as the 1.5 generation, those who arrived in their adoptive countries as a child. When I wrote 'an african american,' that term—African American—was not being widely used, as it is now, as a description of black people in the United States, regardless of their place of birth. Growing up, I recognized that my background, my personal history, was different from most of the other black students with whom I went to school. There were many times when I was teased because I was different, and there were many times when I felt as if I belonged nowhere because I was not fully one thing or the other, not fully American yet not fully African, either. I wrote 'an african american' because I wanted to express the influence of, and my commitment to, the two cultures that I claimed; the two places that I considered home."

NIKKI GRIMES is an award-winning author of books for children and young adults. In addition to *Is It Far to Zanzibar?*, a Parents' Choice Honor book, her works include the popular poetry collections *Meet Danitra Brown*, *My Man Blue*, and the novel *Jazmin's Notebook*. Her teen novel *Bronx Masquerade* won the Coretta Scott King Award, while her biography *Talkin' About Bessie: The Story of Aviator Elizabeth Coleman* was a Coretta Scott King Honor book. Ms. Grimes makes her home in Southern California.

She says, "I went to Tanzania in 1974 to research Swahili language and literature after earning a minor in Swahili in college stoked my interest in African folktales. I traveled to Tanzania and lived there for a year in hopes of finding good tales for translation. My experiences led me to write the book of poems *Is It Far to Zanzibar?*

During my year in Tanzania, I visited the town of Bagamoya, a place that truly got under my skin. There was something unearthly about it, something I tried to capture in the poem of the same name. I don't know how successful I was, but I can tell you this: Once you've been to Africa, its spirit haunts you for the rest of your life."

ANGELA JOHNSON received her first major literary prize in 1991, when her second book, *When I Am Old with You*, was named a Coretta Scott King honor book. Since that time, Angela has won two Coretta Scott King Awards, for the novels *Heaven* and *Toning the Sweep*, and a second Coretta Scott King honor for *The Other Side: Shorter Poems*. Her most recent novel is *The First Part Last*, which was published by Simon & Schuster in July 2003. She lives in Kent, Ohio.

"I visited Africa when I was a teenager. Unfortunately, I only traveled through the northern part of the continent. I always felt I missed something. There was a longing to see, hear, and feel what I had been raised to believe was my family's true homeland. Once, when I was small, I sat watching a documentary on Nigeria, when suddenly, I saw a man who looked so much like my grandfather that I jumped up and screamed. It only came to me years later that my recognition of one face on a huge continent proved how hungry so many generations of children like me must be for a history."

JANE KURTZ is the author of twenty books, many of them connected in some way with Ethiopia, her childhood home. Her first novel, *The Storyteller's Beads*, was a finalist for the PEN West Literary Award. One of her first picture books, *Fire on the Mountain*, was a Children's Book of the Month Club alternate selection. *Only A Pigeon*, which she coauthored with her brother, Christopher Kurtz, won a Parents' Choice Gold Award and the Africa Studies Best Book for Young Readers award. *Water Hole Waiting*, also written with Christopher, was one of *School Library Journal's* Best Books of 2002. Her book about surviving a flood in North Dakota, *River Friendly River Wild*, won the Golden Kite Award for excellence in picture-book text from the Society of Children's Book Writers and Illustrators. She now lives in Kansas, but since 1997 she has managed to travel almost every year to Africa.

"When I was a child in Ethiopia, Eritrea was the northernmost region of the country. Since I lived in the southwest, I only visited Eritrea a handful of times, but

I always found it a fascinating place. While there, I longed to see the shores of the Red Sea, but we had to cancel our family trip to the area because of fighting along the roads. Later, after I returned to the U.S. and the war between Ethiopia and Eritrea had become intense, I spent several years researching the roots of the conflict and the daily lives of people under war. Now I have many Ethiopian and Eritrean friends who live in the U.S. Because of my own childhood spent in the crossroads among several cultures, I'm gripped by their experiences and struggles.

"'Flimflam' is a story that, alas, could take place at almost any time. In the 1960s, the emperor of Ethiopia took Eritrea over as a province. Guerilla fighters in Eritrea struck back. Eventually the tension led to a long war, finally resolved with a vote for Eritrean independence in 1993. But in May 1998, armed conflict between the two countries broke out again over border dispute. Although a new peace treaty was signed in December of 2000 and prisoners of war were finally sent back to their own countries in 2002, tensions remain. The thousands of Ethiopians and Eritreans who fled to the United States during the time of trouble often live with their hearts half in one continent and half in another, while their children—for the most part—simply think of America as home."

SONIA LEVITIN has written nearly forty books, among them the popular Journey to America trilogy. She has written in many genres, from picture books to young-adult novels. One of her most recent books, *The Cure*, combines science fiction with the novelization of a stunning true incident in the Middle Ages. Her much-acclaimed *The Return* was honored with many awards, both in the U.S. and abroad. A mystery novel, *Incident at Loring Groves*, won the Edgar Award, and another suspense novel, *Yesterday's Child*, a combination of history and science fiction, was a finalist for the Edgar Award. In *Dream Freedom*, a novel set in a country torn by civil war and religious persecution, the tragedy of slavery in Sudan is depicted amid scenes of the pastoral, intriguing life of the Dinka people, some of whom she came to know during her research.

"My first encounter with Africa was in second grade, when we were given pictures of giraffes, lions, and elephants to color. I understood that these wonderful creatures were part of a vast, raw, and beautiful place where animals roamed freely, plants flourished, and people lived their lives in intimate connection with nature and the larger universe.

255

I fell in love with Africa, though I would not personally see her. It is an attraction that has lasted all my life. My fascination was enhanced by a friendship with a black child in my grade. Janet and I were inseparable; I liked her style, her ready smile, her confidences. In the early 1980s when I learned that in Ethiopia there lived a 'forgotten' community of black Jews, my fascination went further; I wanted to see these people, touch their lives, learn their stories. The result of my quest was my novel *The Return*, which is the basis for a new musical."

MARETHA MAARTENS is Afrikaans speaking and writes rather laboriously in English. She has written more than one hundred books for children and adults: novels, picture books, a children's Bible, inspirationals, and a biography of Marike de Klerk, the tragically murdered wife of the previous state president of the Republic of South Africa. Several of her books for children and teens, including *Die Invoe (Paper Bird, Ink Bird)*, have been translated into other languages. A literary novel written in 2001, *Jacoba Afrikaner*, was one of the finalists in the Insig-Tafelberg Great South African Adult Fiction competition. Maretha loves cats, a fact that is reflected in her children's book *Midnight Cat*. She and her husband live a simple life in a sunny city in the central part of South Africa. They have spent most of their earnings on travel or on enabling their daughters to travel.

"'The Homecoming' reflects my admiration for Tolkien and my love for the arid, lesser-known regions of South Africa. A friend, who is presently housing ex-exiles, told me about the hardships these highly developed human beings—to use Mr. Nelson Mandela's words—suffer in the challenge to readapt to the harsh S.A. climate, to loss, and newness. I saw the potential for a story.

"South Africa has changed dramatically since 1994, when, after the release of Nelson Mandela, the first democratic election was held. Five million disadvantaged households have been supplied with running water and electricity for the first time in history. Schools have been upgraded. Education for all now forms part of the constitution. Black and 'colored' kids whose parents cannot afford to pay school fees receive free education, which means free books, pocket calculators, and computer training.

"Lincoln has landed *bump!* in the New South Africa. Manfred, his new friend, is a so-called colored person, the largest group of Afrikaans-speaking people in the country. Manfred's great-great-grandmother might have been a black woman and his great-great-grandfather might have been a white man. Before 1994, Manfred's people did not fit in anywhere. They did not fit in with Zulu-, Sotho-, or Xhosa-speaking people, because they speak Afrikaans. They were looked down upon by white people because of the color of their skin. Manfred is a new-generation South African kid. He believes that the past will not be repeated in his lifetime."

ELSA MARSTON has a degree in international affairs from Harvard University and has lived in several countries of the Middle East and North Africa, with frequent sojourns in Beirut. Among her recent books are a novel set in Egypt, *The Ugly Goddess*, and works of nonfiction including *Muhammad of Mecca*, *The Byzantine Empire*, *The Ancient Egyptians*, and *Women in the Middle East: Tradition and Change*. Her stories for teenagers appear in three collections, *Soul Searching: Stories About Faith and Belief*; *Join In: Multiethnic Short Stories*; and *Short Circuits: Thirteen Shocking Stories*. Shorter stories and articles appear in *Cricket* and *Highlights for Children*. "The Olive Tree," set in Lebanon, won the International Reading Association short story award in 1994. She lives in Indiana, where she likes playing tennis.

"Like Dalenda in 'Scenes in a Roman Theater,' I once spent many sunny hours painting the Tunisian country-side for a one-person show in Tunis, sometimes getting hassled by the local kids! At the Roman ruins at Dougga, I bought a straw hat from a young vendor: the kind of hat worn by farmers—and surprisingly becoming. Those good memories date back some twenty-five years, when my husband, a political scientist from Lebanon who specializes in the Middle East/North Africa, was working for the Ford Foundation in Tunis. Tunisia has made much progress in modernization, such as good schools and women's rights, and attracts tourists with its beautiful scenery and magnificent heritage from ancient cultures and medieval Islam. Five centuries of Roman rule left impressive ruins. But tourism can have disadvantages, too, undermining some social values as young Tunisians are lured by money to be made at the large, glitzy resorts. I decided to give Hedi a glimpse of a future that—in the long run—might prove more satisfying to him."

MUTHONI MUCHEMI grew up on the slopes of the Great Rift Valley just after Kenya gained its independence. "Kamau's Finish" is the fourth of her stories to be published in her two-year-long writing career. Before that, she worked in advertising and market research in Nairobi. She currently lives in Cairo, where her husband works for a multinational company. Between them, they have four children. She is working on her first novel.

"Watching television was a luxury my parents allowed only on special occasions, but in the 1972 Olympic Games, my whole family cheered as Kipchoge Keino won Kenya its first gold medal. Kipchoge became a national hero and inspired many to follow in his footsteps. Today, Kenya is the most successful producer of long-distance athletes in the world. 'Kamau's Finish' was inspired by memories of school races where 'Run like Kip!' was the rallying cry."

STEPHANIE STUVE-BODEEN is the author of the Elizabeti's Doll series of picture books, for which she received the Ezra Jack Keats New Writer Award, the Minnesota Book Award, the Paterson Prize, and honorable mention for the Charlotte Zolotow Award, among others. Her newest picture book is *Babu's Song*. Stephanie lives with her husband and two daughters on Midway Atoll National Wildlife Refuge, the northernmost island in the Hawaiian archipelago.

"In 1989 I went to Tanzania as a Peace Corps volunteer.

I came home a different person, changed by the majestic landscape and intense extremes of the country, and the inspiring warmth of the Tanzanian people. My feelings for the beautiful, imaginative children of Tanzania helped to create my Elizabeti's Doll series of picture books. 'What I Did on My Summer Safari' is based on a safari I took with an American diplomat and his family. In reality, there were three children under ten, in addition to the visiting grandmother. It took us much longer to reach the camp after we broke down, and I never thought I would see the situation as anything but awful. But now I can only look back, laugh, and wish I had the words to describe how truly heinous those tsetse flies were."

UKO BENDI UDO grew up in Nigeria, and then attended college in the United States. He currently does freelance reporting for *The Trumpet*, a London-based newspaper, and is an elementary school teacher with the Los Angeles Unified School District. He is also a member of the Society of Children's Book Writers and Illustrators (SCBWI). He lives in Los Angeles with his wife and daughter.

"On March 18, 2002, *CNN Presents* broadcast *Return to Freedom*, a documentary about the rehabilitation of the children kidnapped to fight in the Sierra Leone civil war. For me, it was a riveting and disturbing broadcast for two reasons. First, the brutality perpetuated on the children was unprecedented. Second, one of the languages used in the broadcast was broken or pidgin English, a language widely used in Nigeria, where I was born and raised. Nigeria also shares, to a certain extent, ancestral and cultural ties with Sierra Leone. One of the children profiled in that CNN broadcast was Sasko Simbo, a teenage boy who made sergeant in the rebel army. As I watched, I wondered. How was this boy ever going to be 'normal' again? How much killing had he done as a rebel soldier? Did he have a Nigerian ancestry? How would he fare if he found himself in a far-removed environment like the U.S.? What would happen if he crossed paths with another child with an equally traumatized psyche—for instance, a Los Angeles gang member? To find answers to some of my questions, I read more about the conflict in Sierra Leone. 'Soldiers of the Stone' is my attempt to tackle those questions I found no answers to."

AMY BRONWEN ZEMSER lived in various countries throughout her childhood and adolescence. Her parents taught in American schools overseas, and while many of the places she has lived have been memorable, no other place has affected her quite so dramatically as Monrovia, Liberia, where she spent three years. She has written short stories based on her experiences there, as well as the novel *Beyond the Mango Tree*. Zemser now lives in Park Slope, Brooklyn, where she is working on her second novel.

"'Her Mother's Monkey' is based on a real event, although none of the characters are true to life. In fact, my father hated the monkey, and the monkey knew it. Every time my father came near, it would chatter and scream at him. My mother, though, loved the monkey as if it were her child. She never pretended to hate the monkey, like the mother in the story; in fact, she openly expressed her affection, and years after we had left she still spoke with anguish about the day she had to leave her beloved pet at the zoo. The image of our monkey crying and holding out his hands to my mother through the bars of the cage at the zoo was not an easily forgotten one, and eventually became the driving force for the rest of the story."